Picking up he
Adelle stepped o
threw the shirt o
minute she lay
image invaded h

A blank face in . . . So blank it was barely a face at all. A face shape, then. A disembodied shape. Vague. Disjointed. Hovering way, way back in the mirror. Much further back than any normal reflection. Like a creature lost from its own time and space, suspended in limbo, using the mirror to try to get out . . .

Also available by Sandra Glover,
and published by Corgi Books:

BREAKING THE RULES
'Handles serious issues with a humorous touch...lively dialogue' *Books For Keeps*

'A rattling story. Suzie's battle with officialdom will uplift all who read it' *Yorkshire Evening Press*

THE GIRL WHO KNEW
'Superbly spooky' *Daily Mail*

THE NOWHERE BOY
'Quirky, wise, ingenious...my sort of read'
Robert Swindells

FACE TO FACE

Sandra Glover

CORGI BOOKS

FACE TO FACE
A CORGI BOOK: 0 552 547468

First published in Great Britain by Andersen Press Limited

PRINTING HISTORY
Andersen Press edition published 2001
Corgi edition published 2002

1 3 5 7 9 10 8 6 4 2

Set in 12/14½pt Bembo by FiSH Books, London WC1

Corgi Books are published by Transworld Publishers,
61–63 Uxbridge Road, London W5 5SA,
a division of The Random House Group Ltd,
in Australia by Random House Australia (Pty) Ltd,
20 Alfred Street, Milsons Point, Sydney, NSW 2061, Australia,
in New Zealand by Random House New Zealand Ltd,
18 Poland Road, Glenfield, Auckland 10, New Zealand
and in South Africa by Random House (Pty) Ltd,
Endulini, 5a Jubilee Road, Parktown 2193, South Africa

Made and printed in Great Britain by
Cox & Wyman Ltd, Reading Berkshire

Chapter 1

Adelle leant against the toilet door, breathing softly, hoping they wouldn't notice she was missing. She could hear their giggly voices, beyond the door, in the changing rooms. Monday afternoon, devoted to games, was the highlight of their week. Theirs, but not hers.

It had been easy to get out of games at her old school – the large, anonymous, Yorkshire comprehensive, which Adelle had attended when she'd lived with her gran. There you could forge a note, plead stomach cramps or ingrowing toe nails, or simply hide yourself away somewhere. Nobody ever noticed who was missing.

Six months of miserable experience had taught Adelle that it was different here. At the small, private girls' school which she'd been coming to since her move back down south. Small so she could have more individual attention, private because Dad believed expensive meant better and single-sex to avoid the 'boy trouble' which had happened in Yorkshire.

So here she was, lumbered with teachers who'd be more at home running prisons and girls whose prime hobby was telling tales.

'Where's Adelle, Miss?' she could hear Naomi Gardiner bleating. 'We haven't got a full team.'

'Adelle!' Miss Jarvis called, as she banged on the toilet door. 'Adelle, are you in there?'

'I feel sick,' Adelle called, faintly.

'Nonsense,' Miss Jarvis replied, briskly. 'It's a lovely, crisp afternoon. You'll be fine out in the fresh air.'

Adelle sighed. Emerging from behind the door, she tried to pull her T-shirt down, to cover her thighs. Thighs, which in Adelle's opinion, wouldn't have looked out of place on a slightly obese rhinoceros.

'Come along,' Miss Jarvis urged, handing Adelle a hockey stick. 'And tuck that shirt in. You look a mess. Come on, Adelle. Tuck it in. Honestly, it's not as though you've got anything to hide. Anyone would think you were fat, the way you carry on.'

Sniggers from the girls.

'Very funny!' Adelle mumbled, as they made their way onto the pitch, shivering in the cold, February wind, which Miss Jarvis thought so lovely. 'Well, I'll show them!'

Adelle had once been good at games. Junior school rounders and netball team. Winner of the Year 7 tennis cup, in Yorkshire. But sport wasn't considered cool by her Yorkshire friends. She'd stopped playing. Her weight had crept up. People had started to notice. To make remarks. And since then, she'd taken to avoiding games altogether, preferring to exercise alone. Jogging or dancing to her fitness tape, in an attempt to firm up the flab which refused to budge.

Well, with or without flab, she could hit a ball as well as anybody, she told herself, as she took up her position on the left. Granted, running around was a bit of a strain. But with a few clever tactics she could keep effort to a minimum and still make an impact on the game.

'You really are good, when you get around to playing,' said Naomi, back in the changing rooms. 'Can't understand why you try to skive off so much! I mean, you're good enough for the school team.'

'I'm not a team sort of person,' said Adelle, refusing to be taken in by Naomi's flattery and easy smile.

It would be better if Naomi left her alone, Adelle thought. But there was no chance of that. On Adelle's very first day at the school, Naomi had been assigned to look after her and 'Miss Perfection' took her duties very seriously. She had shown Adelle round, introducing her to people and giving her tips on which teachers to avoid upsetting.

Now, six months on, Naomi was still happily trying to organize her and, whilst Adelle had been grateful for the initial kindness, she'd made it quite plain that she didn't want to get too involved. Not that Naomi had taken any notice.

The trouble was, Adelle thought, Naomi was gushingly friendly with everybody. She was irritatingly flamboyant with masses of striking, red hair and a personality as fizzy as a newly-opened can of Coke.

'Never mind,' said Naomi cheerfully, undaunted by Adelle's glacial stare. 'You're probably wise. Some of the schools we play go a bit mad. Look at this cracker I got last week.'

She rolled down her sock, to display a huge, still purple bruise on her slim ankle.

'Talking of crackers,' she said, glancing anxiously round for Miss Jarvis. 'Has anyone got anything to eat? I'm starving.'

'Keep an eye out for Miss,' said Anna, delving into her bag and bringing out a whole packet of chocolate biscuits. 'Want one, Stella?'

'No thanks!' said Stella, stepping back as if the mere aroma of chocolate carried dangerous, airborne calories. 'You know me. Blow up like a whale if I so much as look at a bikkie.'

She patted her pancake-flat stomach as she spoke and stretched her long, slender legs.

'You'll have one, won't you?' said Anna, offering the packet to Adelle. 'A choccy biscuit or two isn't going to make much difference to you, is it?'

Adelle took two, just to show she didn't care. Just

to show that their jibes couldn't hurt her.

On the way home, Adelle bought four Mars Bars from the shop opposite the bus stop and ate them, one after the other. Feeling gross, guilty and bloated, she knew she couldn't face the three flights of stairs up to the flat and waited instead for the lift.

As usual, at that time in the afternoon, the lift was empty except for mountains of sweet wrappers, discarded beer cans and the overpowering smell of urine, which warned you to be careful where you put your feet. One of the many reasons, Adelle reflected, why she could never invite the girls from school to her mum's flat... even if she wanted to. Her dad's place in London, of course, would be OK but there were other reasons why she couldn't invite them there.

In the empty flat, on the table in the tiny kitchen, sat a note, reminding her that her mother was staying on late, at her school, for a parents' meeting. A note instructing Adelle to help herself to one of the packet meals, with which the freezer was always crammed.

She ignored the message, deciding instead to do some of her exercises to work off the effects of the Mars Bars, before going onto her homework.

The homework took ages, Adelle deliberately drawing it out, to pass the time.

She looked at her watch, as she finally pushed

the completed homework to one side. Twenty past seven. Her mum's meeting, she knew, ended at eight thirty. But Mum wouldn't be home until long after that. First she'd go for a drink with 'Desmond from Physics'.

Adelle wasn't sure what she disliked most about Des. The fact that, at twenty-seven, he was sixteen years younger than Mum or the fact that he was simply the most boring person she'd ever met.

Maybe Mum thought Depressingly Dull Desmond made a refreshing change after Dad, Adelle reflected, as she opened the freezer. And who could blame her, after what Dad had done?

Adelle looked, in disgust, at the packets of low-calorie Chow Mein, Vegetable Lasagne and Chicken Korma which filled the freezer. She took them out, in turn. Examined the calorie counts on the packets, before putting them all back. The Mars Bars still weighed heavily on her stomach and her conscience.

Why had she done that? Why had she eaten them? How could she ever expect to get her weight down if she still gave in to stupid cravings, sometimes? She simply had to try harder. Tomorrow she would really cut down, she promised herself.

Feeling sick and weary, she meandered between the bathroom and her bedroom, eventually flopping down on the bed, staring at the low ceiling, with its flaky paint and thin lines where the plaster had started to crack.

The whole room needed decorating but it wasn't going to happen. There was no money. Mum had refused to take anything from Dad after the divorce, announcing that she would return to teaching. Take care of herself and of Adelle, if necessary. The only exception she made now was Adelle's school fees. Dad paid for those.

At first, of course, her mum had only herself to worry about. After the trouble, four years ago, eleven-year-old Adelle had gone to live with her gran, in Yorkshire, away from the hurt and gossip. In Yorkshire, she'd adopted her gran's maiden name, calling herself Adelle Sheridan to avoid recognition. She used the name, still. People, Adelle knew, can have long memories.

Adelle sat up, allowing her eyes to wander from the ceiling, around the rest of the tiny, bare room with only the basic items of bedroom furniture. Pine bed, cheap built-in wardrobe, low chest of drawers, empty bookcase.

There was nothing of herself in the room. Beneath the bed, books languished in boxes, personal items lay neglected in plastic bags, even most of her clothes nestled in still locked suitcases. And, in a box, carefully protected by bubble wrap, lay something special.

In the first few weeks, after Adelle had left

Yorkshire and come to live with Mum, she hadn't been able to face unpacking anything but the absolute essentials. As the weeks turned to months, she'd thought about it once or twice but had never actually got around to doing it. Unpacking implied acceptance. Acceptance of things she simply didn't want to accept.

It was time, Adelle suddenly decided, getting up from the bed. It was time to stop pretending. Time to face facts. She was here to stay. Her gran was dead. The large, Victorian house in Yorkshire sold. Nothing was going to change that. There was no going back. It was time, as Gran had so often told her, to move on.

Tears blurring her vision, Adelle reached under the bed for the special package. It seemed only right to unpack that first. Gran's gift. The mirror which Gran had left to Adelle in her will, six long and painful months ago.

No ordinary mirror, Adelle thought, as she carefully removed the bubble wrap. An antique for a start. Over two hundred years old. A family heirloom, purchased long ago by her great-great-grandfather. Valuable. Precious. But what made the mirror really special was not its value, but the memories it held. Memories of Gran.

Gran had loved that mirror. Once, it had stood on her dressing table next to a pottery wash bowl and jug. Also antiques. Gran had a passion for antiques. It was the reason she hadn't sold the old house after Grandad died. Or, at least, one of the reasons. There weren't many cottages or flats which could house a ten-foot long sideboard, Edwardian dining table and a grandfather clock. Let alone all the pottery and paintings. So Gran had stayed put, she and Adelle rattling around in a thirty-roomed mansion.

Carefully removing the bubble wrap, Adelle lifted out the mirror. She placed it on the chest of drawers, playing with the stand, tilting it this way and that, until she was satisfied it was at just the right angle.

She'd done the same thing, many times, when she was little, spending the long summer holidays at Gran's. The mirror had always fascinated her, with its smooth, perfectly plain, polished wood stand.

She stared at it, as she used to long ago, touching the silk-smooth wood. Wood which appeared to be an entirely ordinary shade of brown until you looked close. Then you could see shades of red, orange, yellow, even purple, if the light was right. As if, as Gran used to say, the original tree had once captured a rainbow and held onto it, weaving it into its grain which formed shapes like elongated eyes.

Hand-made. Perfectly crafted. Pity, Adelle thought, as she caught a glimpse of her reflection, to spoil it with a vision of something so unpleasant. The flabby-cheeked, puffy-eyed unpleasantness which insisted on gazing back at her.

She pulled a damp tissue out of her pocket and dabbed at her eyes, spreading the blotchy pinkness. Not the desired effect at all. She peered closer, at the faint red lines radiating from her pupils, the dark circles underneath, then gasped as she caught sight of something else. A faint shadow hovering, momentarily, behind her own reflection.

Adelle swung round, expecting to see her mother or, at least, hear her footsteps padding along the hall. Nothing. The room was empty, the door only slightly ajar.

She got up, moving towards the door. She had definitely seen something. A fleeting image. Had someone broken into the flat? Had they hurried past the gap in the door? Were they, even now, lurking in the lounge, the kitchen?

Tiptoeing, quietly, Adelle crept out into the hall. No-one there. All was still. The outside door was firmly locked.

Convinced, yet not convinced, Adelle slipped slowly towards the lounge, peeping into the empty room. She checked the kitchen, the bathroom, her mother's bedroom. She even looked in the wardrobe for hidden intruders. Or, more likely perhaps, Mrs Cropper's cat, Nero, who had, more than once, hidden somewhere before leaping out at Adelle, causing her heart to stop.

Nero, this time, was clearly innocent of attempted murder. The image she'd seen, Adelle decided, was no more than a trick of the light or perhaps a flying insect, whose size she'd exaggerated in her mind's eye.

Still, it was unnerving, she thought, as she wandered back to the bedroom. She'd be glad when Mum got home. She glanced at her watch, once again, before returning her eyes to the mirror.

She was beginning to regret unpacking it. She'd never really been one for gazing in mirrors. Had never thought there was much to look at. Even though people told her she was pretty. Or at least they used to. They didn't say it so often now, Adelle remembered. Not since she'd started to get fat.

But once a mirror is in position, it's hard to avoid. Adelle couldn't resist sitting down, to take one more look, just to see if the puffiness had started to go down. If her cheeks looked any less like a bulging hamster's.

Resting her elbows on the chest of drawers, she leant forward, saw, again, something which wasn't herself, screamed and bolted for the door.

She bumped into Mr Ahmed, who was standing right outside the flat.

'Are you all right?' he asked, turning his head slightly to his own open door opposite. 'I heard a scream.'

He wasn't the only one. The walls of the flats were tissue-paper thin and neighbours were popping up all over the place. The Newson twins, hanging over the banister on the floor above. Mr Ahmed's mother hobbling out. Mr and Mrs Cropper arriving, breathless, from downstairs.

'I . . . I . . . saw something,' Adelle blurted out, to the ever-growing crowd of neighbours. 'In the . . .'

She stopped. How could she tell them what she'd seen? Who would believe her?

'I'm sorry,' she said, aware that she was still trembling. 'I feel such an idiot. I must have had a nightmare. Drifted off in front of the telly.'

'I'm not surprised,' said Mrs Cropper. 'The muck they put on these days. Before nine o'clock and all. Disgusting it is. Is your mum not back yet?'

The YET, emphasising that the night-time parental absences were something else Mrs Cropper found disgusting.

'Er, no,' said Adelle. 'There's a meeting. At school.'

She didn't mention 'Desmond from Physics'.

'Right,' said Mrs Cropper, taking control. 'Come on then, pet. You look terrible! We'll phone your mum.'

Mrs Cropper's fussing wasn't usually something to be encouraged, but Adelle was in no mood to argue. She was in no state to venture back into the flat alone either, with that thing hovering in the mirror. It was hard enough to go back, with Mrs Cropper guiding her, holding on to her arm.

Adelle barely saw where they were going. Barely registered the lounge or the sofa where Mrs Cropper positioned her. All she could think about was the face. The face, or rather, the face shape which had hovered in the mirror. The long, thin, white, featureless face. The alien face which was not her own.

Chapter 2

Fortunately Adelle's mum was still at the school when Mrs Cropper phoned. Alerted by the anxiety in her neighbour's voice, she hurried home, listened to Mrs Cropper's story and ushered her out, muttering apologetic thanks.

'You look awful!' she announced, sitting down next to her daughter who hadn't moved from the sofa. 'What on earth were you watching to have a nightmare?'

'I wasn't watching anything,' said Adelle, bursting into tears, throwing her arms round her mother.

'Adelle, love, what is it? It isn't the girls at school again, is it? What've they said this time?'

'No,' said Adelle, sitting up, trying to control her sobs. 'It's nothing to do with school. I . . . I . . . saw something. In the mirror.'

'Which mirror? What sort of something?' said her mother, in confusion.

Confusion which increased as Adelle tried to explain, first the fleeting glimpse which she'd thought was an intruder, then the dreadful, ghostly face. Totally blank. No eyes. No mouth.

No nose. Yet still a face.

Almost before she'd finished, her mother started shaking her head.

'Oh, no,' she said. 'Oh, no, Adelle. Don't start all this again.'

'I'm not,' Adelle screamed. 'I'm not making it up. It's not like last time. I was a kid then. I was hurt, angry, upset. It's not like that now. I really saw it. It was there.'

'Get the mirror,' her mother ordered.

'I can't. I can't go in there.'

'All right. I'll get it.'

Her mother got up and marched, briskly, out of the lounge, returning, equally briskly, with the mirror. She knelt down beside Adelle, positioning the mirror between them.

'Look,' she said, in her school teacher voice. 'Look, Adelle. Tell me what you see.'

Adelle stared at the double image. Herself and her mother. Nothing more. Nothing sinister. Nothing lurking in the distance.

She hung her head, then looked again.

'I know,' she said. 'I know what you're thinking.'

'I'm thinking what I've always thought,' said her mother, more gently. 'That you've got a very active imagination. An imagination which gets over-excited, stirred up, sometimes.'

'But I wasn't over-excited tonight,' Adelle insisted.

'Oh, Adelle,' said her mother, sighing. 'Just unpacking the mirror. Just getting it out would be enough to set you off. Thinking about your gran, thinking about the old house. The games, the fantasies! Remember what you used to be like when you were little?'

Remember? How could she forget? The excitement of each holiday bubbling up inside her weeks before they set off! The twin feelings of fear and anticipation as they drove up the motorway towards Yorkshire and the detached Victorian mansion which greeted them. A rambling sprawl of rooms and corridors full of mysterious delights and terrible secrets.

Gran had inherited the house, in her early twenties. In it, she'd brought up her three boys, Adelle's dad and his two older brothers, Uncle Alan and Uncle Roderick. Later, when the boys were all married with children of their own, they would bring their offspring and deposit them each Easter, each summer. Sometimes at half-terms, as well. For some fresh Yorkshire air and a chance to run wild.

Adelle barely knew Uncle Roderick's three. In their teens when Adelle was born, they had stopped their holiday visits to Yorkshire in favour of camping trips with friends or backpacking in Australia.

So it was with Uncle Alan's four children, all older than herself, that she had played.

To a toddler, wandering around Gran's house had been like staying in a giant's castle. Vast rooms. Ornate ceilings, miles high. Dark furniture, brooding and massive.

Memories of playing hide-and-seek with her cousins came flooding back, as she sat with her mum, gazing at the mirror.

Memories of crouching under a huge four-poster bed. Heavy feet crunching towards her. Knowing they were too heavy for Amanda or Nick. Shivering as she saw the tips of black, leather boots. Holding her breath, so he wouldn't hear. Knowing that if the giant caught her, she'd be popped into the cavernous oven downstairs, baked and eaten. Scaring herself to death with morbid imaginings!

The mirror, in fact, was one of the few things in her gran's house that she'd considered completely harmless. That didn't hide something dark and menacing. The coloured jars and bottles in the bathrooms harboured genies. The painting, of the lady in blue, had ghostly eyes which followed you round the dining room. If you looked at her while you were eating, the food turned to wriggling worms in your mouth. Or so Mark had told her.

Then there was the goblin in the cellars which made it unsafe to venture there alone. The chest at the top of the stairs, which Adelle had never dared open after Amanda had told her there was something inside, scratching away, clawing to get out.

The way you had to open the door of the garden shed at arm's length and drag your bike out before the spider dropped. Adelle had never actually seen it but Julia had insisted it was the size of a small cat.

Adelle found herself smiling. Laughing out loud.

'What's so funny?' her mother said.

'I was just thinking,' Adelle said. 'About my cousins' games. No wonder I've got an active imagination, as you put it! Remember that summer, when I was five? When Nick and Julia woke me up in the middle of the night, getting me to creep downstairs, in the dark, to count the chimes of the grandfather clock. They counted with me, right up to 13! The magic hour, when they said the ghosts came out. I woke the whole house with my screams!'

'That's better,' said her mother, as Adelle laughed again. 'All those spooky, supernatural fantasies that your daft cousins filled your head with were just that. Fantasies. But you took them all so seriously.'

Dead right, Adelle thought. In fact, she'd never dared confess to her mother how deep it had all gone. That not once, even when she was older, even when, at the age of eleven she went to live with Gran, had she ever ventured into that cellar alone or raised her eyes to the lady in blue.

'So I reckon,' her mother was saying, 'that getting the mirror out brought it all back. Set you off imagining again. You were probably remembering some mad tale they'd told you about the mirror once.'

'I don't think there were any tales about the mirror,' said Adelle, thoughtfully. 'I don't remember any.'

'Not consciously,' said her mum. 'But I bet they once told you about a long, pale face in the glass.'

Her mother put on a silly, spooky voice as she spoke, making Adelle laugh again.

'So we'll put the mirror back,' said her mother, convinced the crisis was over. 'And I don't want to hear any more nonsense about faces.'

Later, as Adelle settled down to sleep, her mother popped her head round the door.

'No brooding,' she warned. 'Think about something pleasant before you go to sleep. I always imagine I'm on a nice warm beach somewhere, with the sun blazing down on my back and an ice cold gin and tonic in my hand.'

Beaches were a bit hard, for even Adelle's active imagination, in the middle of February, with the heating still turned down low to save money.

So instead, as her eyes started to close, she went back in time and place to the house in Yorkshire. Not dwelling, this time, on the creepy games she played with her cousins but on the pleasant ones she played on her own, when she could escape into the old nursery in the attic.

There she would ride on Bess, a Victorian rocking horse with a red saddle and soft, silver mane. There, also, she would play with the dolls' house. The same one that her gran had played with, when she was little. Four storeys high, like the real house, it had a dozen rooms filled with hand-made, miniature furniture.

Best of all, was the Smiddles – the family of dolls who lived in the house. Mother, father, three children and the maid who wheeled the baby out in the black pram with the white cotton pillow.

The pretty maid doll used to be her favourite. She'd made up lovely stories about her, until Cousin Julia had ruined it by telling a grim tale of her own. Adelle couldn't remember the details but it was nasty enough to have spoilt her games.

Spoilt. Everything was spoilt now. Thinking about the attic was a bad move. Happy memories rapidly gave way to sad ones, as Adelle began to focus on the attic as it might be today. Slowly turning into a poky bedsit which would, in the future, smell of stale smoke and spilt beer. The whole house had been bought by a property developer who was converting it into flats.

'We can't be fussy who we sell to,' practical Uncle Roderick, the lawyer, had said. 'Nobody wants these big houses these days. Too expensive to maintain.'

Adelle had hoped against hope that someone in the family would take it on. But Uncle Roderick was right. They all preferred to live in their modern boxes and nobody wanted to live in Yorkshire. Except her.

The haste to sell the house and most of the antiques had, in Adelle's opinion, been indecent. The day after Gran's funeral, six months ago, Adelle had sat in tears, as aunts, uncles and cousins squabbled over the will.

Nick, moaning because money for the grandchildren had been put in trust until they were twenty-five. Mark gloating because that, in his case, was barely more than a year away. Nineteen-year-old Amanda throwing a toddler-like wobbler because Julia had been left a sapphire ring, while Amanda herself had to make do with a painting. Make do! The painting was an original. Worth a fortune. Hardly something to whine about.

What they hadn't realized, what they perhaps hadn't even wanted to see, was that Gran, in the final weeks of her illness, had thought very carefully about her last gifts. Amanda had been given the painting as a hint, to get herself off to art college. She was a talented artist was Amanda, but she'd done nothing except doss around since leaving school.

Julia's ring had been a hint, too. A hint that she should accept Geoffrey's proposal. Gran thought Geoffrey was a steady young man, who had steered

Julia away from the drug crowd she'd been mixing with.

Maybe the hint had sunk in, in Julia's case, Adelle thought, because she and Geoff had just announced their engagement.

And what of her own gift? The mirror? There'd been a reason for that too. A reason she didn't want to think about. Adelle shook her head, trying to push the thoughts to the back of her mind, where they belonged. Trying not to hear, again, what Gran had told her, only a week before she died.

Adelle glanced over at the mirror. Shuddered at the half-remembered conversation and the thought of what she'd seen. She *had* seen something. And if she'd seen it, if it was real, it might be there still. How was she expected to ignore it? To sleep with it in the room?

Picking up her school shirt from the floor, Adelle stepped quickly towards the mirror and threw the shirt over it. It didn't help much. The minute she lay down and closed her eyes, the image invaded her mind.

A blank face in a mirror. So blank it was barely a face at all. A face shape, then. A disembodied shape. Vague. Disjointed. Hovering way, way back in the mirror. Much further back than any normal reflection. Like a creature lost from its own time and space, suspended in limbo, using the mirror to try to get out . . .

It was too much for Adelle. She leapt up, grabbed her duvet, scurried into the lounge and made herself an untidy cocoon on the sofa.

Even then, sleep refused to come, driven away by the questions. Had she really seen a face? And if so, who was it? What was its source, its nature, its purpose? By the time her mother's alarm clock began its high-pitched wail, at six o'clock the following morning, Adelle thought she had the answer.

Chapter 3

'I'm worried about Adelle,' Naomi Gardiner informed her friends.

'Well that's no great surprise,' said Anna, dismissively. 'Who don't you worry about? One of the juniors who's looking a bit lost, a stray dog, a wasp with a damaged wing? Anybody and anything! I mean, you fretted more about my mum's operation than I did myself. Nearly drove me nuts!'

'I know,' said Naomi. 'I stick my big nose in where it isn't wanted. But it's better than ignoring things, isn't it?'

'No,' said her friends, together.

'So you think I should leave Adelle alone?' said Naomi. 'To skulk around being miserable, day after day?'

'How do you know she's miserable?' Stella asked.

'Oh, come off it! She's been here six months, never speaks unless she has to, refuses all invitations . . . I've tried to get her involved in things but she just doesn't want to know.'

'Exactly!' said Anna. 'She's a loner. Loads of

people prefer their own company. We can't all be raving extroverts, like you, thank goodness! Adelle's quiet, that's all. It doesn't mean she's unhappy. Just leave her alone. She'll settle, in her own time.'

'Yeah,' said Naomi. 'But I feel sort of responsible. The Head told me to look after her!'

'For the first couple of weeks,' Anna pointed out. 'Not for the rest of her life, for heaven's sake! You've done what you can. Now back off. Let Adelle be herself. She'll join in when she wants to.'

'But it's not just that she's anti-social,' Naomi insisted. 'It's other stuff.'

'Like what?' said Stella, sighing.

Everything, Naomi wanted to say. Almost everything about Adelle was odd. The way she hardly ever looked anybody in the eyes. The way she hunched her shoulders, as if she was carrying a massive sack of rocks. Not to mention the most obvious problem of all.

'Well, her weight for a start,' Naomi said. 'Have you seen . . ? '

Naomi stopped, as Adelle appeared in the doorway and wandered past them to the seat at the back which she had made her own.

'Idiot,' Anna hissed, fuelling Naomi's blushes. 'She heard you. That's not going to help much, is it?'

Naomi turned, trying a brief, apologetic smile in Adelle's direction before Mr King strode in and claimed their attention.

He didn't manage to claim much of Adelle's. Her eyes were almost shut, her mind adrift in a haze of missed sleep. She hadn't wanted to come to school. It was four days since she'd seen the face in the mirror and the following restless, tormented nights had left her exhausted.

She'd kept the mirror covered, like a disruptive parrot in its cage. But it hadn't helped. One day, one day soon, Adelle knew she'd have to look again.

Something had disturbed her. Something more than the appearance of the face itself. Something she'd thought about night after sleepless night. The familiarity. The shape, featureless as it was, had seemed familiar. As if she was supposed to recognize it. Like when you pass someone on a crowded street and they smile at you, briefly, before walking on. And you spend ages afterwards, racking your brains, wondering if you were supposed to know them, from somewhere.

'Open your exercise books, please.'

The message filtered through and Adelle dutifully opened her book, though the rest of the instruction was no more than a blur of words, as if Mr King had suddenly taken to speaking in Chinese.

Copying the rest of the class, Adelle picked up her pencil. It hovered above her book, doing nothing in particular, as her mind returned to her private thoughts. Crazy thoughts. Thoughts that the shape in the mirror might be a spirit, an imprint, a ghost. A ghost of someone she knew. Someone who had a reason for trying to contact her.

'Adelle! What on earth are you doing?'

Mr King's voice, and his hand snatching her pencil away, jolted Adelle back to reality.

She followed the teacher's gaze to her book. To the page where she'd been drawing. A page covered in pictures of long, blank faces.

'I'm sorry,' she managed to mutter, before bursting into tears.

Mr King looked round, helplessly, as if hoping to prove that his harsh tone hadn't been responsible for this outburst.

'I'll take her to the medical room,' Naomi volunteered.

Later, in her bedroom, Adelle approached the mirror.

She'd managed to shrug off Naomi's concern, telling her it was no more than girls' problems combined with the onset of a cold, which had set her off snivelling. That the blank faces in her book were merely an artistic interpretation of her own boredom.

The school nurse had been a bit trickier. She'd droned on about the importance of getting plenty of sleep and of sensible eating. She'd given Adelle a couple of leaflets and scribbled a letter for her to take home to Mum. Three documents which were now safely shredded into the bin next to the bus stop.

Adelle had read the letter before destroying it, of course. It was asking Mum to make an appointment. No hassle. She'd already dealt with that. A letter written on the lap-top, thanking the nurse for the leaflets, assuring her that everything was under control at home and that Adelle's mum would certainly be in touch if there were any future concerns. A forged signature had finished it off. Tomorrow, Adelle would post the letter, but for now, the mirror was her prime focus.

She knew she had to confront it. She would have to look again. Not scream, this time, or bolt from the room, but take a really close look.

Whipping the shirt away, quickly, like a stage conjurer, Adelle sat down on the edge of the bed and stared, unblinking, into the glass.

Catching her breath, she stared, in horror, at what she saw. Not a pretty sight. Pale, podgy, puffy, porky. An albino piglet complete with pink eyes. That was how she saw herself. Only herself. There was nothing beyond. Nothing behind. No shapes. No faces.

She was almost disappointed. At least the face would have been a distraction. Something to take her mind off her own repulsive reflection. The nagging reminder that however hard she tried, her diet just wasn't working.

As she stared hard at the mirror, Adelle heard her mother move across the lounge to switch on the news. Adelle ignored it until the voice of the newscaster began to sound more animated, turning from the European Parliament to something a little juicier. A little closer to home. A footballer had been dropped from his Premier League team after some unsavoury allegations which he insisted were untrue.

Adelle, no football fan, didn't know the player but she wondered whether he had a wife, a family. She knew how they'd be feeling. How she'd felt when her dad had hit the headlines four years ago.

She got up and wandered out to the lounge doorway. The news had moved on. An accident on the motorway, caused by people driving too fast in icy conditions. Mangled cars. Mangled lives.

Her mother turned off as it moved on to education.

'I can't listen to that,' her mother snapped. 'Another new initiative from the government. More bits of paper to fill in. As if we haven't got enough to do! Sorry, love. Did you want something?'

'Just to say goodnight.'

'Sleeping any better?' her mother asked with a deceptively casual tone.

'Yeah. I'm fine now.'

She would be too, now that the face had gone, Adelle told herself as she curled up, clutching her hot water bottle with the furry frog cover. The one Gran had bought for her a few years ago, when Adelle had been plagued by nightmares. Frog's silly, protruding eyes and wide, stupid grin were supposed to make her smile, help her relax, before she went to sleep. Surprisingly it had helped. It still did. Frog provided warmth, comfort and memories of Gran, all in one.

Even later, when she woke, Adelle felt no alarm, at first. Waking in the night had become commonplace. She groped around for Frog, who'd slithered down the bed, but as she held him close, she had the sudden, urgent feeling that she wasn't alone.

Switching on the bedside lamp, Adelle sat up and looked, expectantly, towards the door. Her mother, too, was a light sleeper and often paused, in the bedroom doorway, to look in on Adelle, on her way to the loo.

She wasn't there. Yet still Adelle could feel eyes upon her. Could sense a presence in the room.

It was coming from the mirror.

As surely as if it was calling her name, Adelle knew it was there.

Getting up, she edged her way along the bed, towards the end, towards the mirror.

She knew she shouldn't. She knew she didn't want to. It was the same feeling she got each and every time she passed a cake shop, crammed full of cream cakes and sticky delights.

Irresistibly, she would be drawn in, emerging with a carrier bag full of goodies and the sickness of guilt in her churning stomach. These days, she wouldn't even eat the cakes. She'd give them to friends or dump them in a waste bin somewhere. But the sickness would linger.

The nausea was there now, as her eyes were sucked towards the mirror. In the half light she saw first herself and then the face.

Did she force herself to watch or was she already transfixed, unable to avert her eyes? The shape seemed a little further forward than it had been before. Changing, even as she watched. Like a white fluffy cloud, in a pale sky, taking the form of a mountain or a dragon. Breaks and lines appearing to make rivers or gaping mouths and flailing tails.

Such lines were etching themselves on the face. A straight line, the hint of a mouth. Curved lines, arched like eyebrows over vague, unseeing eyes, which shifted position. Wavy lines of fine, wispy hair.

The pretence of watching nothing more than a cloud lasted only a moment. No cloud this. Not a reassuring sky but a smooth expanse of glass, reflecting an image without a source.

Throwing herself face down on the bed, Adelle tried to stifle a scream and the sickness which welled in her throat.

'Adelle, for goodness' sake, what's going on?' her mother shouted, bursting into the room, switching on the overhead light. 'You'll wake the whole block!'

'I'm sorry.'

'It's OK,' said her mother, putting her arm round her.

'No,' said Adelle, 'I saw it. I saw it again. The face. It was there again.'

'You had a nightmare,' her mother said wearily. 'A nightmare, that's all.'

'It wasn't a nightmare,' Adelle insisted. 'It was there. I saw it.'

'Is it there now?' said her mother, picking up the mirror, forcing Adelle to look.

Adelle shook her head.

'It's not there all the time,' she said, lamely. 'I looked earlier and there was nothing.'

'And when it comes, if it comes,' said her mother, 'what do you suppose it is? What lurks in a mirror one minute but not the next?'

Adelle had to smile, in spite of herself. It sounded like one of those daft Christmas cracker riddles.

'I don't know. I thought . . . I thought.'

'Go on, spit it out.'

'Ghost,' Adelle blurted out. 'It's like something, someone, from another world, trying to get back.'

'Ghost,' her mother repeated. 'This is the twenty-first century, Adelle, not the Middle Ages! There aren't any ghosts. They don't exist.'

'How do you know that? How do you know? If you'd been really close to someone. If they had a reason for coming back . . .'

'This isn't just any old ghost you're talking about, is it?' said her mother, beginning to catch on. 'You think it's something to do with your gran, don't you?'

'It could be. I know it could,' said Adelle. 'There's something I haven't told you. Something I haven't told anyone. We had a row, Gran and me. The week before she died.'

'But you and Gran never argued. Not ever!'

'We did, that day,' said Adelle.

'What on earth about?' her mother asked.

'It doesn't matter,' Adelle snapped. 'It's not important. She was trying to tell me something, that's all. I wouldn't listen. I just started shouting. Stormed out. I really upset her, Mum. When she was ill and everything. So isn't it possible . . ? '

'No,' said her mother firmly. 'No, it isn't. Listen to me, Adelle. Your gran was a wonderful person, yes?'

Adelle nodded.

'And she loved you?'

Adelle nodded again, wondering where this was getting them.

'And did she ever hurt you, in any way, ever in her life?'

'No!' Adelle said.

'So she wouldn't want to hurt you now, would she?' said her mother, triumphantly. 'Even if she could come back, which she can't, love, she wouldn't do it this way! She wouldn't lurk in a mirror, scaring you half to death, just to finish a conversation! It's all in your mind, Adelle. You've conjured up the ghost because you feel guilty about the row, maybe.'

'But it's so real,' said Adelle, quietly.

'A real fear, maybe. A real sense of guilt. Nothing else. There are no ghosts.'

It sounded so straightforward. So clear cut. So logical. It was pointless to say the words Adelle wanted to say. The words which filled her head over and over.

'But I saw it. I saw it.'

'I'll take the mirror into my room,' her mother said. 'Just for a day or two, till you feel better, OK?' Then, a little quieter, almost to herself, 'I wonder if we ought to go back to the doctor?'

'No!'

'She could maybe give you something to calm you down.'

'I am calm!' Adelle screamed, forcing a laugh from her mother.

'It's not just these hallucinations,' her mother said carefully. 'I think we ought to go back, anyway, about your weight.'

'Oh, don't you start. I've had enough of that at school!'

'So the girls have been saying something?'

'It doesn't matter. I don't care what they think.'

'They're probably concerned about you, love. Like I am,' her mother said softly. 'Perhaps we ought to take up the doctor's offer of counselling.'

'No,' Adelle said, again.

'There's no shame in it,' said her mother. 'Lots of people have counselling, these days, for all sorts of things.'

'Dad, for example,' said Adelle, bitterly. 'For his little problem.'

'Yes and it's helped,' her mother insisted. 'It could help you too. Think of the stress you've been under! Gran dying, moving back down here, new school that you hate . . .'

'No,' Adelle screamed. 'I don't hate it. I'm getting used to it. I'm coping. I'm not seeing any doctors and I don't need counselling. I'm in control. I'm not crazy.'

Words to join the others in her head. To be repeated over and over throughout the night like some religious chant.

'I saw it. I'm not crazy. I saw it.'

Chapter 4

'Doing anything special, this weekend?' Naomi asked.

'No,' Adelle lied, reluctantly shuffling up so that Naomi and Stella could join her on the bench in the garden.

The school didn't have a playground. It had gardens with lawns, ponds and pathways, bordered by trees and shrubs. Just a touch different from her old school with its bleak tarmac and high perimeter fence.

Nobody ran around here. Not even the juniors. Nobody screamed, fought or played. They sat or walked, exchanging gossip, inventing secrets.

Anna wandered up, bringing out a packet of sweets, offering them round. Adelle shook her head and put her hands in her pockets to avoid the temptation.

'Adelle says she isn't busy this weekend,' said Naomi, pointedly.

'Oh, good,' said Anna, though without much enthusiasm. 'Mum's changed her mind about my birthday. She said I couldn't have a party or anything because of having my bathroom and bedroom completely redecorated but now she says I can take a few friends out for a pizza on Sunday. So can you come?'

'No,' said Adelle. 'No I can't, I . . .'

What excuse can you make when you've just been tricked into saying you weren't busy? Adelle said the first thing that popped into her mind.

'Er, I can't, I daren't. I've started a new diet.'

She saw Stella's lips twitch as she and Anna exchanged glances. Naomi's eyes flicked, critically, towards her.

'Adelle,' she said bluntly. 'I don't want to be personal or anything and I know it's none of my business but, I mean, what exactly do you weigh?'

'Wow!' said Stella, as Adelle got up and walked off without a word. 'You sure have a way of putting your foot in things, Naomi. Tactless or what?'

'I was trying to . . . this weight business with Adelle . . . I was trying to help!'

'Oh, very helpful,' said Anna, flopping into Adelle's vacated seat. 'Look at her! She looks really happy now, doesn't she?'

Adelle was standing, some distance away, by the small pond, her back to the girls, head down, shoulders hunched.

Why couldn't they just leave her alone? She'd convinced herself that things had been getting better recently. At school and at home. It was almost Easter. Nights were getting lighter, the weather brighter. She'd been feeling cheerful, optimistic.

Memories of her last 'blip', as her mother called it, were beginning to fade. After the vision, the hallucination, nightmare or whatever, she'd avoided the mirror for a while. Left it in her mother's room. Then, gradually, she'd plucked up courage to look again. Had seen nothing more interesting than the lopsided parting in her blond hair or a tiny spot on her forehead.

She used the mirror daily now. No problems. The two isolated incidents almost forgotten. Dismissed as tricks of the light. Tricks of the mind. Brought on by stress. Guilt. The pain of missing Gran.

Mum had, eventually, given up talk of doctors and counsellors, her attention drifting away from Adelle, back to work and Desmond. Adelle didn't mind. She enjoyed the freedom to be herself without her mother fussing about what she was eating and whether her homework was finished.

Her work had, in fact, been getting better. Almost back to its old standard. And she'd been coming out of her shell a bit more too. Making an effort to talk to people, Naomi especially. She was OK was Naomi, if you ignored all the surface gush and fizz. They had a lot in common, shared similar tastes in music, books and films. All of which they discussed with the same offbeat humour. Naomi made her laugh, distracting her from morbid thoughts.

Being around Naomi, Adelle reflected . . . somehow made her feel more confident. Reminding her of how she used to be . . . popular, outgoing, at ease with herself. And Naomi had a way of getting her to talk about things, without actually brooding. She'd even started to tell Naomi bits about her family. The safer bits anyway. Her aunts, uncles and crazy cousins.

Adelle had started to talk about her grandparents too. It had felt good to open up, just a bit. To let Naomi into her life. So why did Naomi have to go and spoil it? Why did she have to mention weight?

The bell summoned Adelle away from her thoughts, back towards the school for the last two lessons of the week. A couple of hours would see the start of the weekend. The last weekend in March.

The last weekend of each month was marked, in black, in her diary. A time to be dreaded. A time, whenever possible, to be avoided. The visiting-Dad-in-London weekends.

The visits had started six months ago, after Gran had died. After Adelle moved back down south. In Yorkshire, she'd been safe. The distance was judged too great for regular access, the shock of what her dad had done, too recent.

Once in her mum's flat in Bedfordshire, distance had ceased to become a problem. And, after a space of four years, the pain was supposed to have gone.

'You're fifteen. You're old enough to understand, now, Adelle,' her mum had said. 'What your dad did wasn't so very dreadful, you know.'

Oh, but it was. Dreadful enough to have reduced Gran to tears, time and time over, when she thought no-one was around. To prompt Grandad to go off to the golf course shortly after the story broke, saying he needed to get out, relax, forget. He never came back.

Everyone said that the heart attack was in no way connected. That it would have happened anyway. But the coincidence loomed too large for Adelle. She blamed Dad then. She blamed him still.

Not to his face, of course. There was too much love left to want to hurt him more. Love stemming from a time, long past, when she was small and Dad was her hero. They had been proud of each other, then. So many of her best, early memories seemed to involve Dad.

Dad reading *Paddington Bear* in a silly, squeaky voice. Dad making a snowman in the garden and pulling her along on a red, plastic sledge. Dad taking her to the zoo where she perched on his shoulders, trying to stare into the eyes of a young giraffe. Giggling when it stretched out its rubbery tongue and tried to lick her face.

When had it started to go w
Dad started to spend less time at h
they started to grow apart?

Sometimes, when Adelle was feelin
in control, she would take out her ph
album and lie on the bed, flicking over e pages full of her dad's near professional prints and her own childishly haphazard snapshots.

Herself, her parents, grandparents, aunts, uncles and cousins would all gaze up at her. A giant game of happy families. Happy, rich, successful families. Uncle Rod, the lawyer. Auntie Wendy, the accountant. Their daughter, Fiona, the vet. Their sons both computer consultants.

Uncle Alan and Auntie Elaine, college lecturers with their four children bright and clever. Adelle herself, pink and clean in her ballet costume or grubby and unkempt on the lawn at Gran's. A little on the chubby side, perhaps, but still pretty.

Then the star. It took some effort to shine in a family like hers. But Dad had managed it. His brothers had been prefects at school. Dad became Head Boy. Several members of the family had University degrees but only Dad had First Class Honours from Oxford. There were photos of Dad with sports' trophies, Dad with certificates, Dad with prizes.

Everyone had been proud of him. No-one in the family resented his successful career. No-one

..en he threw it away. His family rallied ... support. Put on a brave face. Certain that ..ad was down but not out.

It seemed that they were right. After a year or two working mainly abroad, Dad was back. Not as prominently as before. Working behind the scenes, rather than in the limelight. But his career, he confidently predicted, was about to take off again.

That, amongst other things, was what filled Adelle with dread. If she could, she would plead illness and postpone her visits. Last month, the face in the mirror had been her excuse. Unnerved. Unsettled. Unstable. Her mum had agreed she was in no fit state.

Two postponed visits in succession weren't allowed, so on Saturday morning, Adelle was bundled onto the train by her mother. Condemned until late on Sunday night, when Dad would drive her back.

'Send my love,' her mother urged.

Adelle knew she meant it. Despite everything, there was a part of Mum, a part of herself, that loved him still.

Adelle waved and settled in her seat, trying to quell the feeling of sickness in her stomach and the burning acid in her throat. She hoped that her dad hadn't arranged one of his little 'treats'. A visit to an art gallery, the theatre, or worse, a plush restaurant, where she would keep her head down and her eyes firmly glued to her plate. Too terrified to eat. Scared of being seen. She would much rather spend the weekend, quietly, at his flat.

It seemed funny calling Dad's home a flat. It was far too posh. Nothing like her mum's place. It was big, for a start. Part of a converted house in what estate agents call 'a desirable area'. One where nobody would dream of dropping sweet wrappers or urinating in the lifts.

Just in case, there were security cameras all over the place, a surly caretaker and a daunting series of locks and intercoms to keep out unwelcome visitors.

She was far from unwelcome. Her dad was always gushingly grateful and pleased to see her.

He strode towards her the minute she got off the train. He was far too tall, too striking, too handsome. At 47, with silver hair and immaculately tailored suits, he was, unfortunately, the kind of person that was noticed. Eyes, mainly female, were drawn to him now, as he stopped in front of her, sheepishly offering a carrier bag.

'I bought these for you,' he announced. 'Tracked them down in an antique shop.'

Adelle let her dad take her overnight bag in exchange, while she peeped in the carrier, rustling layers of tissue paper to reveal six little dolls and a miniature pram.

'The Smiddles?' she said, barely able to believe it.

'Well, I know you're a bit old for dolls,' he said. 'But you seemed so disappointed that they'd been sold with the rest of the stuff, I thought I'd buy them back for you. I thought about getting the dolls' house as well but you probably wouldn't have room, in the flat.'

'No, these are lovely. Honestly,' said Adelle, almost dropping the bag, as she tripped.

'Are you OK?' he asked, catching her arm. 'You look . . . very pale and your mother said you hadn't been too well.'

'No. I'm fine. Tripped over my laces, I think. That's all.'

Her dad looked down at her feet, frowning as she bent to fasten the offending lace.

'Those trainers are a bit of a mess. Tell you what. How about we do a bit of shopping? Get you some new ones?'

The word 'shopping' froze Adelle, as surely as if someone had popped an ice cube into her heart. Her instinct was to shout, no. To point out that Mum had promised to get her new trainers next week. That there was no need.

But there were trainers and trainers. The ones her mum could afford came from El Cheapo Shoe Mart. The sort she wouldn't dare let the girls at school see her wearing.

Greed began to burn, melting the ice. There was a residential trip coming up, at school, soon. A trip she couldn't possibly sign up for unless she had the right clothes.

She would only have to mention it and the offer of trainers would swell to include jumpers, trousers and a jacket. All bought from the very best places. Money no object. Her dad was always keen to make amends for the poverty which, he said, her mother inflicted on herself and Adelle. Dad would buy clothes so expensive that they'd almost disguise her many failings and bodily imperfections. Baggy sweatshirts. Loose jackets.

There was no contest. Avarice outweighed her fear of being seen. Dumping her bags in the back of Dad's Mercedes, they set off.

Adelle was so caught up in the frenzy of purchase that she almost, no totally, forgot who she was with. Her dad became no more than an anonymous hand which presented the bank card, attached to an arm over which bags could be hung.

Then, from behind a rack of trousers, came a voice.

'Hi, Adelle. Fancy seeing you here.'

Three figures appeared: Naomi and two other flame-haired females whom she politely introduced as her mother and sister.

They all stood expectantly, waiting for Adelle to do the same. To introduce the man with the carrier bags. But Adelle simply stared, like a wild deer faced with a rifle, her mind racing, inwardly cursing.

How many people were in London that day? How many shops did they have to choose from? What twisted coincidence had brought Naomi here, at the very same moment as herself?

Then more serious questions. Was that glint in Mrs Gardiner's eyes one of recognition? Was introduction unnecessary? Did she already know? Had she remembered?

Adelle found herself clawing at her dad's arm, like a hyperactive toddler.

'We've got to go,' she said, to nobody in particular. 'I'll miss my train.'

Turning, without another word, she bolted from the shop, racing along the street, hoping she was heading for the car park.

'Adelle,' said her father, making long strides to catch up. 'Adelle, what's going on? Who was that? Why were you so rude?'

'I want to go home,' was all she said.

'Why?' he asked, bewildered. 'Don't you feel well?'

'I just want to go home, that's all.'

'OK, we'll pick up the car and . . .'

'No. I'll take my things and get the train.'

'I can't let you go back on your own, the state you're in!'

'I'll get the train,' Adelle insisted.

She watched her dad standing bemused and dejected as the train pulled out of the station.

He didn't know, she thought, as tears began to form. He really didn't know how she felt.

Couldn't he imagine the conversations?

'Was that a friend from school, darling?' Mrs Gardiner would ask Naomi. 'Only that man she was with . . . I was sure I recognized him. Rather unsavoury business, a few years ago. You don't think it could be a relative, do you? Her father, even? What did you say her name was?'

Sheridan might confuse them. Put them off the track. But on Monday, Naomi, in her tactless way, would be sure to ask questions. Girls would gather round, waiting for answers.

Adelle was so wrapped up in her fears that she almost missed her station, staggering off the train just in time. Her legs were shaking so much, she barely managed to drag herself outside to the taxi stand.

The flat was empty, when she got home, as Adelle knew it would be. Her mother was taking advantage of her absence to go off somewhere with 'Desmond from Physics'.

She stumbled into the bedroom, throwing her bags on the floor. Grabbing a tissue she sat on the edge of the bed, leaning forward to wipe away the mascara which had leaked into her eyes, making them sting. That was all she intended to do. All she intended to see. But it was there again. The face. Grinning at her. Growing stronger all the time.

Chapter 5

Stress, Adelle told herself. Panic attack. The wheeze in her chest, the trembling limbs, even the face she thought she could see. All classic symptoms.

Keep calm. Keep breathing. No need to be frightened. Nothing really there. Not real.

It didn't even look real, Adelle tried to tell herself, keeping her eyes fixed on the image.

The features were clearer than before. Much clearer. But still not solid, somehow. They had a two-dimensional quality like a badly drawn pencil portrait.

It was as if her own pudgy reflection had become transparent, allowing her to see beyond. The face, the pencil sketch face, had developed more shape. No longer stretched and alien, it had a strongly defined, prominent little chin and high, angular cheek bones.

Confront it, Adelle told herself. Don't look away. Words her gran had once said came back to her.

'Confront your fears, Adelle. Stand up to them. Look them straight in the face.'

Words that took on a strangely literal meaning as

she looked at the mouth which had grown from a mere line to a harsh fullness, parted in a humourless grin. And the narrow eyes, no longer shifting, which had settled, uncomfortably, on either side of a bony nose.

It was female. Definitely female. Young. Not fully mature. Gaunt. Thin. Not entirely well, Adelle found herself thinking.

She tried to examine it, as she would a picture hanging in a gallery. That's all it was. A picture. A mind picture. But of whom and why. . ?

Suddenly the eyes moved. No more than a blink. Changing the game. Changing the rules. This wasn't supposed to happen. If you confronted your fears they were supposed to fade, go away. Not blink at you, lazy and mocking.

'No!' Adelle screamed, leaping up, stumbling over her bags in her race for the door.

She darted into the bathroom. Hastily bolting the door, dropping to her knees, grasping the side of the loo with both hands. Desperate to clutch hold of something solid. Something tangible. Something real.

In the lounge, the phone was ringing. On and on. Almost certainly Dad, checking to see if she was home safe, Adelle thought. Home, yes. Safe, no. But there was no way she could tell him. No way she could unlock the door. No way to get help.

Later, much later, the sound of a key in the door.

Voices. One low, boring. The other high-pitched, irritatingly flirtatious.

'I can't stay long,' Des muttered. 'I've got all that marking to do.'

'Can't it wait?' Adelle heard her mother say. 'I'm not expecting Adelle back till late tomorrow. I thought we might at least have dinner. Well anyway, fix us a drink while I pop to the loo.'

Door handle turning. Faint tap on the door. Louder banging.

'Adelle! Adelle, is that you? Des! Come and use some of your muscle. I think the door's stuck.'

Time to come out. Time to open the door before Mr Muscle broke it down.

'It's me,' Adelle announced, rather unnecessarily, as she stumbled out.

'Adelle! What on earth! What are you doing here? You look awful. What's happened? Adelle?'

Mum nearly fell over with the sheer force of Adelle hurtling towards her, clutching her tight, sobbing hysterically.

'I'd better go,' said Des, obviously anxious to escape.

Neither Adelle nor her mother registered his departure. They were already moving towards the lounge.

'Adelle,' said her mother firmly, as they sat down. 'Stop it, now. Stop this nonsense. You've got yourself into a right state! Tell me what you're doing home. Why aren't you with your father? What happened?'

'I . . . I . . .'

Adelle didn't want to confess. Barely dared say that she'd seen it again. But the memory was too powerful, the terror too strong.

'The mirror,' she began.

'No!' said her mother. 'No excuses. No silly stories about the mirror. I want the truth. And if you're not going to tell me, I'll phone your dad.'

Giving Adelle no time to respond, she picked up the phone, rattling off questions. Where had they been? What had they done? What had been said? Had anything unusual happened? Why was Adelle home?

'Yes, I know she's uptight,' her mother screamed down the phone. 'Yes, I've noticed the weight. No, we haven't been to the doctor's. You know what she's like! She won't even talk to me about it, let alone a doctor! She goes hysterical if I so much as mention the word! Anyway, that's not the point. I want to know what happened today.'

She paused, waiting for answers, sighing deeply, before coming back to sit down.

'So you bumped into a friend?' she said, understanding what Adelle's dad had failed to understand.

'Yes but . . .'

'And you panicked?'

'Yes but . . .' Adelle tried again.

'Listen, love,' said her mother. 'You've got to get a grip. Surely you're old enough now to realize that what your dad did was pretty tame compared to what some people get up to? I know it was tough for you, for all of us, at the time but these things blow over. There's been a million scandals since then. If people remember, it will be no more than a vague recollection of something which barely matters any more. You can't keep getting yourself into a state.'

'I don't care about that!' Adelle yelled. 'Well, yes I do. Of course I do. But that's not why I'm in a state, as you put it. I saw it again, Mum. I saw a face in the mirror. Three times, now, I've seen it.'

'Adelle!' said her mother, almost out of patience. 'Stop it! You're not a child any more. You can't keep hiding behind these games of make-believe. Creating imaginary terrors to mask the real ones. Terrors you believe will grab people's attention. Force them to listen to you.'

'It's not imaginary,' said Adelle, weakly. 'Not this time.'

There was no chance, Adelle knew, of her mother believing her. But it wasn't like the last time, Adelle was sure.

Last time, she'd been just eleven years old. Packed off to Gran's to avoid the scandal she barely understood. The things people were saying about her dad, the strain it had put on her parents' already dodgy marriage, were still a tornado of grief in her mind when, within a month of her arrival in Yorkshire, the next tragedy hit. Grandad's death. The heart attack on the golf course.

She had flipped. No doubt about it. Phoning her mother in the middle of the night to describe the thin, grey wolf which haunted her dreams. Screaming for Gran to search the bedroom for the huge rat with yellow teeth which gnawed at her while she slept or to banish the bird with enormous wings and razor-sharp beak which tapped on her window.

But she was over all that. She'd seen a doctor, taken tranquillizers and learnt some breathing exercises to keep her calm. In the end, though, her recovery had nothing to do with doctors and their stupid pills. It had been Gran who'd saved her with her endless patience and soothing voice. Driving away the demons, real and imagined. Helping her to understand the confusions of the grown-up world.

Gran, Adelle knew, had put aside her own grief, in order to help her. And it was for Gran that she'd tried to be stronger. She'd settled down. Coped. Even functioned at school. Maybe not as well as she'd done before all the trouble. Maybe she hadn't quite lived up to family standards, but she'd done enough to please the teachers and get reasonable reports. She had tried desperately hard, not wanting to upset anyone further, not wanting to let Gran down.

OK, she admitted to herself, so things had changed slightly, when she'd started going out with Steve. She'd fancied him for ages. All the girls did. But she'd never thought she stood a chance. He was two years older than her, for a start, and Year 11 boys simply didn't lower themselves to go out with Year 9 girls.

Yet, somehow, Steve had noticed her. Said she was the prettiest girl in the school and she was hooked! For the next six months Steve was all that mattered. Steve liked pubs and parties and laughed at her when she said she didn't drink and had to be home by ten thirty. He teased her about being 'a kid' and goaded her into joining in, staying out late. But that was as far as it went. Just the usual things teenage girls got up to. Gran had kept a quiet eye on her. Gran had understood.

Mum was a different matter. She met Steve once, on one of her rare visits north, and went hysterical. He was a yob, a waster and what was Gran thinking of, letting dear little Adelle stay out till all hours, caked in make-up and wearing a skirt that looked like a belt?

Mum phoned Dad with news of what she called 'boy trouble'. There was talk of sending Adelle to boarding school. More rows. More conflict.

All the things Adelle had tried so hard to avoid.

Anyway, Adelle thought, bitterly, they needn't have worried. All the aggro was for nothing. Steve had dumped her, shortly after that. Turned round one day and told her she was getting boring . . . and fat. Within hours, she'd seen him draped round Jasmine with her spidery legs and thin, ferret face.

There had been no more boyfriends since Steve. Not many friends, either, for that matter. At first, she'd started a diet, carried on going to parties, tried to get Steve back. But it was hopeless. She'd started to withdraw. Then, once her gran got sick, Adelle had stopped going out altogether. Her naturally outgoing nature had become subdued, so that now she found it difficult to socialize at all.

Not that Adelle cared. Her gran had been more important to her than friends, more important to her than anyone. She'd wanted to stay in, wanted to help. She would have done anything to avoid losing her gran. But the illness had been too far advanced. There was nothing anybody could do.

Adelle felt her mother's arm on her shoulder and realized they were both crying.

'I'm sorry,' Adelle said. 'I don't mean to cause any more trouble.'

'I know,' said her mother. 'I know.'

The mirror was removed again. Locked away, this time, in her mother's wardrobe.

If she ignored it, Adelle believed, if she forgot it was there, her problems would be over.

For a while, it worked. Adelle's fears about what the Gardiners might or might not know subsided. Naomi made no mention of their meeting in London. Bubbly as ever, she chattered on about *EastEnders* and the fortunes of Arsenal, making Adelle laugh with her impersonations of actors and players.

Amused by Naomi and comforted by her mother's logic, Adelle meandered through the next two weeks studiously avoiding all thought of the mirror, watching the most banal TV soaps, quizzes, and chat shows to block out thoughts.

She took to concentrating harder in lessons, stuffing French verbs and parts of flowering plants into the gaps in her mind. And she made a more determined effort with her diet, compiling a scrapbook of food, with calorie values neatly listed, to remind herself of what she mustn't eat.

All the time she mechanically answered her mother's daily questions about her health, her food, her weight, until the start of the Easter holidays, when the questions started to fade and all that remained were her mother's pitying glances. Glances which spoke as clearly as words: 'What have I done to deserve a lunatic for a daughter?'

It was the TV programme which set Adelle off again. An apparently harmless chat show, which she had on in the background while she was sticking some magazine pictures onto the front of her scrapbook. Pictures of some nice, slim, Jasmine-like people to remind herself what she was aiming for.

Barely listening, something caught Adelle's attention. A man was being interviewed. A man who claimed to have seen a whole regiment of Roman ghosts up on Hadrian's Wall, whilst out, one evening, walking his dog. The terrified dog had bolted, leaving the man to watch as the spectral soldiers marched by.

He was mad, of course, Adelle decided. Only he didn't seem mad. In his late sixties, a retired engineer with no previous history of mental problems, he had begun to write a book about his experience and was contacting others who claimed to have witnessed the paranormal.

There was no shortage of volunteers. Several were in the studio audience.

One woman had undergone a series of operations on board an alien spacecraft, showing a tiny star-shaped scar, behind her left ear, by way of proof.

Then, there was the young boy whose parents claimed he was a reincarnation of the Egyptian Pharaoh, Rameses. Only five years old, the boy seemed to know an awful lot about Rameses. And he spoke Egyptian!

'Frauds,' Adelle muttered to herself, as another

woman stood up, to explain how she could cure people by touch alone.

But, somehow, they didn't seem like frauds or loonies. They answered the host's snide questions with patience, sincerity, even humour. Drawing Adelle in.

If those people were telling the truth, if the unexplained existed still, in defiance of twenty-first century science, then maybe her mirror really did hold a secret . . .

Proof. What she needed was proof. An airline pilot, on the TV, was handing over a photograph. Blown up on the screen, it appeared to show a spacecraft.

Photos, of course, the host was pointing out, could be faked.

Adelle switched off. She already knew what she was going to do. Her photography had come on a bit from when she was little but she wasn't advanced enough to be able to fake anything. If she could get a picture of the thing in the mirror, her mother would have to believe her, wouldn't she?

Mirror photography was tricky but possible. Adelle had tried it once, in a mad moment, with Steve, both of them grinning into his bedroom mirror, camera poised. OK, so it hadn't worked brilliantly but you could just about tell who it was supposed to be.

Adelle collected first her camera, then the

mirror. It wasn't difficult to claim it back, from her mother's locked wardrobe, the key having obligingly been left in the door.

She didn't look in the mirror, as she carried it back to her room. It probably wouldn't work. There'd probably be nothing there. Perhaps she shouldn't even try. Perhaps she'd be better leaving well alone, as her gran used to say.

The terror, the memories, had begun to pass. Why was she dredging them up again? Why not simply put the mirror back, before her mother came home?

Because she wanted her mother to believe her, for once. To take her seriously. To help her. That was why.

She sat down, slowly, carefully, breathing deeply to avoid the panic which would surely come, if she saw it again.

It was as if the face had been waiting. Like a spider in a web, patiently waiting for its prey, with the same, menacing intent.

The thing that shocked Adelle, which made her momentarily lose her grip on the camera, was not that it was there but that it had grown.

Not in size but in depth. It was stronger, somehow. More solid. Still like a portrait but as if a better artist had touched it up. Made it more real. Given it . . .

Emotion.

The face had a sadness about it which hadn't been there before, the mouth still with its mocking smile, the eyes downcast and pained.

All these thoughts passed through Adelle's mind in an instant. Banishing all fear, she focused on her task. Pointed the camera.

Click. Click. Click.

Three shots in rapid succession. Best to be sure. After the third shot, Adelle realized that the face had gone.

Chapter 6

'It's no good,' Naomi told Anna. 'I'm going to have to say something about it. I've got to talk to her.'

'There's no point,' said Anna. 'You've tried before.'

'Usually with disastrous results,' said Stella. 'After one of your serious little chats, the poor girl goes right back into her shell. Just stick to nice, normal, everyday topics, Naomi. She's OK when you do that but if you mention weight . . .'

'I've got to,' said Naomi. 'Look at her. She's getting worse. Goodness knows what she's been doing to herself over the holidays.'

It was the first Monday back after Easter. Lunchtime. And Adelle still hadn't spoken to anybody. Naomi had tried at break but Adelle had just turned away. Not rudely but vacantly, as if she hadn't heard.

'She honestly doesn't look much different to me,' Stella said, looking over to the bench where Adelle was sitting, alone, playing with the contents of her lunchbox.

'Come off it,' said Naomi. 'And it's not just the weight, anyway. She looks like a zombie. Haven't you noticed her eyes? They look all sort of glazed.'

'Drugs?' said Anna. 'D'you reckon she's doing drugs?'

'I don't think so,' said Naomi. 'She's real anti-drugs. Told me her cousin had a problem a while back. I can't see Adelle getting involved, somehow. I reckon . . . I think, it's more sort of psychological. Something to do with home. Family problems. Something she's not letting on about.'

'She's not letting on,' said Anna, 'because it's probably private and she doesn't want people prying into her business! I mean it's nothing to do with us, is it? She's not even a friend . . . exactly.'

'School assemblies are wasted on you, aren't they?' said Naomi, scathingly. 'Talk about closing your eyes and passing by on the other side.'

'Watch out,' said Stella. 'Naomi's been swallowing Bibles again. And you can tell she wants to be a psychologist, can't you?'

'It's nothing to do with Bibles,' Naomi protested. 'Or wanting to be a psychologist. I'm not practising on Adelle, you know!'

'Aren't you?' said Anna.

'No! I'm just worried!'

'Listen,' said Stella. 'If there was something wrong, something really wrong, somebody would be doing something, wouldn't they? Didn't you say the nurse was on to it? Didn't she give Adelle a letter to take home, that day you took her to the medical room?'

'Yeah,' said Naomi. 'But it doesn't mean the letter ever got home, does it? Do you think I should have a word with Nurse? See if she's followed it up?'

'Sure,' said Stella. 'She'll be really pleased to have some Year 10 girl telling her how to do her job.'

'Well, maybe I should have a word with one of the teachers.'

'You won't be telling them anything they don't know,' said Anna. 'They're not all as dim as they look! I know for sure that Miss Jarvis is worried. She's probably spoken to Adelle's parents already.'

'Yeah,' said Naomi. 'And what if everyone assumes that someone else is dealing with the problem, when nobody actually is?'

'Oh, come on!' said Anna. 'Her parents'll be doing something, even if school isn't. I mean, she's bound to be seeing a doctor for the weight problem. It's probably glands or hormones or something.'

'I'm not sure,' said Naomi, wondering how much to let on to her friends. 'I get the impression that her parents are a bit preoccupied with their own lives. They're not together, you know.'

'So?' said Stella. 'What does that prove? My parents aren't together but it doesn't stop them fussing about me. In fact, it's double trouble. I've only got to sneeze and they're stampeding over each other to drag me off to the surgery.'

'I know,' said Naomi, remembering her mother's comments that day in London. 'But there's something odd about Adelle's set-up. I mean why did she live with her gran for four years? She talks a bit about her gran but not once has she said why she was living there or where her parents were, at the time.'

'Oh no,' said Stella, laughing. 'You're not lapsing back into your Famous Five stage, are you? You haven't found a mystery to solve?'

'No!' said Naomi. 'Look, I'm going over. Stay out of the way. Let me talk to her on my own.'

'Whoops,' said Stella, as Naomi started to wander down the path. 'Poor Adelle.'

Adelle tried not to notice as Naomi sat down beside her. The only sign she gave was to cover up her lunchbox. Adelle hated people to see what she was eating.

'Hi,' said Naomi, deliberately loud and effusive.

Adelle turned her head, managing a brief smile.

'Had a good holiday?'

No, Adelle wanted to scream. No, I haven't.

The photographs hadn't come out, for a start. Collecting them from the chemist, Adelle had torn open the packet. There were pictures that she'd taken over a year ago, of her old school and Gran's house. Souvenirs of Yorkshire! Then a few hasty snaps of her mother which Adelle had taken to use up the film. And three hazy blurs with the developer's stickers on them, recommending techniques to avoid further disappointment.

'We got to Portugal in the end,' said Naomi, trying not to be put off by Adelle's silence. 'Remember I told you about Dad losing his passport before the holiday and how Mum was flapping around trying to sort out a new one?'

Adelle nodded and smiled.

'Well, luckily, he found the old one. In the greenhouse of all places! Behind his geraniums. I mean what was it doing there? Who needs a passport to visit their own greenhouse? Did you go away?' Naomi added, trying to get something more than a vague smile from Adelle.

'No,' said Adelle, forced into polite response. 'No, I stayed home.'

Stayed home, poring over the three blurs, examining them through a magnifying glass, hoping to catch even the hint of an image. But she couldn't tell Naomi that.

'I, er, caught up on some work,' Adelle said. 'So how was it then? Portugal?'

If Naomi was going to hover, as it seemed she was, it was best to keep her talking about something harmless, Adelle decided. She didn't have to listen.

She could go back to her own thoughts. Thoughts of the mirror and the increasing hold it had over her.

After the disappointment of the photographs, she'd had to go back. Again and again. At first, locking the mirror safely back in her mother's wardrobe each time, then, towards the end of the holiday, leaving it out on her chest of drawers.

It wasn't that the image had gone. That the mirror had become safe. It was simply that Adelle had got used to it.

'Typical, isn't it?' said Naomi.

'Sorry?' said Adelle.

'Of families. You go on holiday and all you do is argue. Everyone wanting to do different things.'

'Oh, yes,' said Adelle.

'Happens every time,' said Naomi cheerfully. 'I suppose I should be used to it by now.'

Funny what you could get used to, Adelle thought. Like Cousin Fiona, when she'd first started to train as a vet. Crying at the sight of every ageing pet which had to be put down and every stillborn lamb. It was getting to Fiona so badly, she thought she'd have to give up. But, no. In time she learnt to cope.

Fiona said it still hurt, even now, but she could distance herself. Focus on the successes. The grateful pet owners who left the surgery clutching their three-legged moggie. One leg short of a full cat, but still, mercifully alive, thanks to Fiona's skill.

Reporters in war zones, or young soldiers, had reported similar feelings. Eyes, at first averted, learn to rest on the atrocities, the mutilations. Hearts and minds come, somehow, to accept the unacceptable.

Was that what had happened to her, Adelle mused. Had she started to accept the face as part of her reality? Accepting that sometimes it wasn't there, yet at others, it would loom firm and strong. And when it loomed, she no longer screamed or ran away. But would sit, sometimes for hours, staring at it, like a picture in a gallery, wondering what the artist was trying to say.

That, Adelle decided, was how she had come to terms with it. By thinking of it as merely a picture, projected through an unusual medium. Only, slowly, it was becoming less and less like a picture. It had started to make her do things. It was starting to take over.

'Adelle,' Naomi was saying. 'Are you all right? You've gone really pale and I don't think you've heard a word I've been saying. It doesn't matter,' she added hastily. 'It wasn't very interesting.'

'I'm not in control,' Adelle whispered.

'Sorry?' said Naomi.

'I'm not in control, any more.'

Naomi stared, bewildered, for a moment. She'd had times, in her own life, when she hadn't felt in control. When teachers were on at her to improve her grades, when her parents were pressing her to practise her instruments, wear less make-up or change her boyfriend. More seriously when her brother was in a car accident, two weeks after passing his test and she'd watched him, for months, in his hospital bed, knowing she was powerless to intervene.

But somehow, Naomi knew that Adelle didn't mean ordinary, everyday sort of out of control.

Carefully, carefully, Naomi told herself, well aware of her tendency to say the wrong thing, to see her 'helpful' comments turn, unintentionally, into armed missiles, from which people ran for cover.

'What do you mean?' she said, as gently as she could.

'Do you believe in the supernatural?' Adelle found herself blurting out.

'I don't know,' said Naomi, measuring her words, watching for reactions, waiting to see if she was getting it right. 'Some things, yes, I suppose so.'

'Ghosts?' said Adelle.

'Maybe. I mean I've never seen one. Don't know anyone who has. Not personally. But there've been some pretty convincing accounts. Why?'

'Nothing,' said Adelle, pulling back. 'No reason. I just wondered.'

Haunted. The word sprang into Naomi's mind. That was the word she'd been looking for when she'd been talking to Stella and Anna about Adelle. The glaze in Adelle's eyes, the pallor, the furtive glances and the way she'd slunk around school all morning. As if something nasty was following her around.

'Adelle,' said Naomi, already sure she was going to make a mess of it. 'I'm sorry. I know I'm a bit blunt and tactless sometimes but that's just me. I mean, what I'm trying to say is... we could talk... if you've got a problem. I wouldn't go spreading it around or anything. Not to anybody. Not if you didn't want me to.'

Tempting, Adelle thought. Naomi looked, sounded, sincere enough. And she needed to talk to somebody. Mum was out of the question. Her dad impossible. But if she told Naomi, would Naomi think she was mad? Would it spoil whatever friendship they already had going? Adelle was surprised to find that she cared. She hadn't realized how much Naomi's bubbly presence had come to mean to her. Was it worth the risk?

Maybe, Adelle decided, she should test Naomi out. Try her on some ordinary secrets and confidences. See how she reacted. See whether they got around. And whether Naomi would start to back off.

'I can't really talk at school,' Adelle ventured. 'But if you'd like to come round one night . . ? '

'Great!' said Naomi, eagerly, thrilled by this breakthrough. 'That'd be great. When?'

Adelle immediately regretted making the offer, tried to settle on some vague point in the future, but Naomi wasn't going to let the opportunity slip that easily. Wednesday, she insisted. Wednesday would be a good day.

There were no good days, any more, in Adelle's opinion. But maybe it was better to get it over with. To let Naomi see the flat, at least. That would probably be enough, in itself, to put her off.

Naomi, however, didn't seem the slightest bit put off, on Wednesday evening, ignoring the graffiti scrawled on the entrance walls and not so much as wrinkling her nose in the lift.

'It's a bit of a mess,' said Adelle, ushering Naomi into the kitchen. 'Mum's saving up for some new fitted units.'

'You don't need to apologize,' said Naomi. 'Not all the girls at school live in dead posh houses, you know.'

'Yeah,' said Adelle, unconvinced. 'But I bet they don't live in slums like this either.'

'I reckon you're a worse snob than I am, on the quiet,' said Naomi, laughing. 'If you think this is a slum.'

'You sound just like my mum,' said Adelle. 'She's forever telling me that people live in much worse places.'

They took their drinks and a packet of biscuits into Adelle's bedroom and put some music on.

'Hey, these are nice,' said Naomi, wandering over to the window-sill, picking up one of the dolls which perched there. 'All hand-sewn little clothes and everything. They're gorgeous. Not like dolls, at all. More like miniature people. Where did you get them from?'

'They were my gran's. They're ages old.'

'I can see that,' said Naomi. 'I bet they'd be worth a fortune now! Sorry. I shouldn't say that. My mum always says it's common to reduce things to their value in money.'

'I don't know how much they're worth,' said Adelle, remembering how her dad had bought them back for her. 'But I won't ever sell them. Sentimental value and all that rot! The Smiddles are . . .'

'The Smiddles?' said Naomi, laughing. 'Was that your gran's name for them or yours?'

'Mine. I made up all their names. Apart from Lucy, the maid. Lucy. . .'

Adelle paused. Lucy hadn't always been Lucy. Adelle had called the maid Kylie until Cousin Julia had intervened.

'Don't be stupid, 'Del,' Julia had said. 'She can't be Kylie, can she? Kylie's a modern name. And this, in case you hadn't noticed, is a Victorian maid. And her name's Lucy.'

'Lucy was the name of a real maid, I think,' Adelle told Naomi. 'Cousin Julia told me a horrible story about her once. But I can't quite remember. Probably wasn't true. My cousins were always making up daft stories about things that went bump in the night. I was younger than them and a dead easy target. I swallowed the lot! Ghosts, ghouls, goblins, giants. You name it and my cousins had a story about it.'

It was so easy talking to Naomi, Adelle thought, as she chattered on. Too easy, especially on home ground. She kept having to think, to stop herself from blurting things out. Talking about the Victorian house, her cousins and the spooky stories, without mentioning why she eventually went to live there. Telling of her grandparents' deaths whilst avoiding all reference to her dad.

Naomi kept wandering round the small room as they talked, picking up books, or clothes that had been left lying around.

'Nice jumper,' she would comment, holding it up to her chest, as if comparing sizes. Or . . . 'I've read that. Thought it was a bit gory. Gave me nightmares! Good though.'

It was only a matter of time, before her eyes came to rest on the mirror.

'I like this,' she said, perching on the end of the bed. 'Good heavens!'

Adelle's heart stopped, the way it did when Mrs Cropper's cat leapt up at her. What had Naomi seen? The face? Was it there? Was this her proof?

'Look how the light catches this frame,' Naomi said. 'The colours in it! Incredible. Have you noticed?'

'Oh,' said Adelle, disappointed. 'Yes. I've noticed that.'

'Are you OK?' said Naomi. 'You've gone pale again, like at school. I keep thinking you're going to faint on me.'

'I think I'm hungry,' said Adelle, opening the biscuits.

Later, Naomi was surprised at the tiny amount Adelle ate, over dinner. She'd only nibbled a corner of a biscuit. Hardly enough to put you off your meal! Yet Adelle's mum seemed not to notice Adelle pushing her food around her plate. Pushing some of it right onto the floor!

She must be worried, Naomi thought. My mum would be doing her nut, if I played with my food like that and then ended up looking like Adelle. What's going on?

The evening didn't bring any answers. Adelle hadn't revealed much that Naomi didn't already know. She'd made no mention of the mysterious problem. Of not being in control. Although desperate to know more, Naomi hadn't pushed it. She'd decided to take Anna and Stella's advice to go slowly. Let Adelle open up in her own time. Only then would she start to get some answers.

Chapter 7

Adelle couldn't wait for Naomi to leave. The evening had gone all right, but Adelle needed time alone before bed. Time to look in the mirror.

It had become like a drug to her. A fix. During the holiday, when she'd felt the obsession becoming too strong, she'd tried hiding the mirror away. But she'd become listless, restless, sick even. She had to go back. She couldn't leave it alone.

Not until she knew. It was like doing a crossword puzzle. Trying to fit everything together. Being frustrated by one last clue, unsolved.

Adelle had solved part of the mirror puzzle. She knew what the image wasn't. It wasn't a figment of her imagination and it wasn't anything to do with her gran. As the face had become clearer, Adelle had got out all the old photos. The really old ones. From one of Gran's own albums. Pictures of Gran as a young woman, her face plump, pretty, cheerful, open. Nothing like the face in the mirror.

Not that the face was always the same. Like a human face, an ordinary face, its expressions changed. Meandering between sadness, fear and worse . . . much worse . . .

Its eyes locked onto hers now. Resentful. The image never spoke. How could it? But Adelle was never in any doubt how it was feeling. Sometimes it teased her with wicked playfulness, fading, withdrawing, then bursting back, stronger than ever. Tonight, though, was not a playful night.

'I'm sorry,' she found herself saying. 'I was busy! I had a friend round.'

The image winked at her, slowly, slyly, mockingly.

'Friend?' it seemed to say. 'You don't deserve any friends. You're too fat and stupid and boring to have friends! Remember Steve?' it silently taunted.

'Who are you?' Adelle whispered. 'Why are you doing this to me? What do you want?'

The face became agitated. Frustrated. As if she were supposed to know.

She had got used to it responding to her voice. One of the many crazy, at first terrifying things she had come to accept. It still made her feel sick, still sent her nails digging into her palms but she could sit and face its anger. She no longer had a choice, in fact. It was as though the face was using her, controlling her, becoming part of her.

Adelle stretched out her fingers, as she had done, only once before, allowing them to brush the glass.

Suddenly her hand pulled back and with one dramatic sweep, knocked all the make-up, brushes, dolls and mugs off the chest of drawers.

The bedroom door burst open.

'Are you OK? I heard a noise.'

Her mother paused, surveying the debris on the floor. Her brow furrowed in confusion. This was the second time something like this had happened in under a week. The first, Adelle had dismissed as an accident.

'I'm sorry,' Adelle was saying, stooping to pick up the Smiddles, first. 'I don't know what's happening to me. I'm getting so clumsy.'

'Adelle, that's not clumsiness,' her mother said. 'You couldn't have knocked all that lot onto the floor by accident.'

'So what if I did it on purpose?' Adelle snapped. 'It's my stuff, isn't it? My room. My mess.'

Her mother looked at her quizzically.

'I'm not worried about the mess. I'm worried about you. You seemed to have had such a good evening, with your friend coming round. She seems like a nice girl.'

'Well, that's all right then, isn't it?' Adelle snapped. 'That's why you sent me to that school, wasn't it? So I could make some nice friends. But what if I don't want nice friends? What if I don't want to be a nice girl?'

'Adelle,' her mother tried again. 'This isn't like you. Just recently you've been so . . . so aggressive. Why can't you just tell me what's wrong?'

'Because you wouldn't believe me,' Adelle

screamed. 'You never have. You never do. So why don't you just get out and leave me alone? Go on. Get out!'

Adelle's head slumped, as her mother left the room. Mechanically, she began to pick up the rest of her things and replace them, haphazardly, on the chest of drawers, looking in the mirror as she put down the last few pieces.

'You did it!' she accused. 'You made me do that.'

The face smiled its twisted smile, the eyes glinting.

'Why?' Adelle asked. 'Who are you?'

The eyes looked down and slightly to the left. Adelle followed the direction of their gaze. Past the hairbrush, the mug, the doll . . .

Adelle picked up the doll, with its black dress and white apron over the top. The Lucy doll. The maid doll.

She held it up to the mirror. Seeing its reflection. Doll reflection. Adelle reflection. And the face. The grinning face.

Adelle pulled the doll back, slightly, away from the mirror. The face followed it, greedy-eyed, as she experimented, moving the doll around, this way and that.

'The doll?' she whispered. 'You like the doll? You want the doll?'

She put it down. Picked up another doll. The man. The Mr Smiddles doll.

The face changed immediately. Becoming dark and angry. So angry that Adelle's eyes burnt in pain and the doll fell from her grasp.

Recovering, she tried the lady doll. The two children. No reaction. Then the baby in the pram.

The face seemed to loom towards her, as if it were going to burst right out of the glass. Adelle leapt up, onto the bed, crouching, terrified, the pram still clutched in her hand. Her eyes had left the mirror only for a moment but when they looked again, the face had gone.

Adelle stayed hunched, breathing deeply, feeling tears cascading from her eyes.

Lucy doll. Mr Smiddles doll. Baby doll. They were all in some way connected. Connected to that thing in the mirror. But how? The dolls hadn't even been in the flat when the face had first appeared.

She'd been talking about the dolls, earlier, to Naomi. Trying to remember a story. But which story? And what, if anything, did it have to do with the mirror? Had something lodged in her mind, all those years ago, to suddenly come back and haunt her? And if it had, why couldn't she remember properly?

Adelle remembered most of her cousins' spooky games, but not all. Sometimes, at family parties, someone would say 'Remember when we told 'Del about the vampire and she painted that cross on her bedroom door and hung up some garlic so it couldn't get in!'

She wouldn't remember the details, though she might vaguely recall Grandad being angry about a bit of painting she'd once done. She'd laugh with them, never letting on how much they'd frightened her.

If there had ever been a story about the dolls, one which still lurked in the depths of her subconscious, then her cousins would remember it. It would be an easy enough thing to ask. To check out. One more clue to follow and probably eliminate.

Slightly reassured, Adelle stretched out on the bed with a pile of magazines and her diet scrapbook. There was no point going back to the mirror. The face hadn't returned. These days Adelle didn't need to look. She knew, instinctively, the minute it was there. And, when it came, there was no ignoring it.

No ignoring the knock on the bedroom door either. Adelle didn't answer but the door opened anyway. Her mum came in and sat on the edge of the bed, a tray balanced in her hand.

'I've brought you a milky drink and a sandwich.'

'I don't want anything.'

'I thought you might be hungry. I noticed you didn't eat much at dinner, again.'

'I did!' said Adelle. 'I ate more than half of it.'

'Just have the drink then.'

'It's milk,' Adelle shouted, sitting up. 'It's full of calories. What's the point of me trying to keep my weight down, trying to look nice again, if you're trying to make me get fatter?'

'Adelle, love,' said her mother. 'You're not fat.'

'Don't lie!' Adelle said, her voice rising to a scream. 'I'm not a kid. Or an idiot. I know what I look like.'

Adelle stared down at her legs, to confirm her viewpoint. She'd always been what people termed 'well-built' but she'd really started to put weight on when she'd moved to Gran's. Partly because Gran was a brilliant cook who insisted people ate regular meals, but largely because Adelle had turned to chocolate and cakes as a comfort.

It was only after the comments in games lessons, after Steve had dumped her, that she had taken a good, long look at herself and realized he was right. She *had* got fat. She'd launched on her diet immediately, started to exercise more but it hadn't made any difference. The flab simply refused to budge.

'I don't think staring at those magazines helps,' her mother was saying. 'Constantly comparing yourself to those models.'

'I'm not comparing myself to anybody,' said Adelle. 'I just want to look . . . normal.'

'And what do you think is normal?'

'Why all the questions all of a sudden? Why all the concern? You never bothered when I was at Gran's. You didn't care about me then!'

'That's not true,' said her mother. 'You know it's not. We, your dad and I, did what we thought was best for you. I came to see you.'

'To moan at me! To pick holes in my reports. To make a fuss about Steve.'

'That's not true. I came because I missed you. Because I love you.'

'Big deal!'

'I wanted you with me, Adelle. I always did. But you were happy there. You didn't want to come back.'

'Too true,' said Adelle. 'I wish I never had.'

The sound of vibrating glass on metal ripped through Adelle's head.

'I'm sorry,' she said, looking down at the tray, unstable in her mother's trembling hands. 'I don't know what's happening to me. Why I say these things. It's not me. I don't mean to. I'm not in control.'

The words had come out again, as they had with Naomi.

Not in control.

She hadn't meant to say them. But it was true. She wasn't. The face was. Even when she couldn't see it. Even when she was nowhere near the mirror, she could feel it with her. Almost all the time, now. Making her say things she didn't want to say. Do things she didn't want to do.

But she couldn't tell her mother that. Not without talk of counsellors and doctors rearing up again. And what could they do? They wouldn't believe her.

'I'm tired,' she told her mother. 'I'm going to have a bath and an early night.'

No-one would believe her, Adelle thought, as she lay back in the water. How could she tell anyone? How could she even have thought of telling Naomi? What did she expect her to do? How could Naomi possibly help?

But then again, Adelle decided, suddenly optimistic, just having Naomi around was a help in itself. It had occurred to Adelle, more than once, that she might have conjured up the face as a sort of bizarre imaginary friend. OK, so she was a bit old for that sort of thing. It was usually toddlers who had imaginary friends. Companions who suddenly departed when the child went to school or playgroup and made proper friends.

So, if she worked on the relationship, opened up a bit more, let Naomi get close, then maybe, just maybe, the imaginary friend would be banished by the real one.

Adelle wasn't convinced that it would be so easy but the next couple of days brought renewed hope. There were no snide remarks or veiled glances from the other girls. No hint that Naomi had said anything about the flat. Naomi herself had been bright, friendly, cheerful as ever, infecting Adelle with her good humour.

On Thursday evening Adelle hadn't even looked in the mirror. She didn't have to. She knew from the calm atmosphere of the room that the face wasn't there.

By Friday she'd decided that soon she would venture a little further. She accepted an invitation to spend Saturday round at Naomi's. An acceptance which served a double purpose. It was the end of the month already. A visiting-Dad-Saturday. But neither of her parents complained when she said she wasn't going. Both were relieved, as she knew they would be, that she was socializing again. Mum was positively falling over herself to encourage the friendship with Naomi.

The only complaint came from the face. Late on Friday night, after she'd phoned her dad, her room became hot, stifling, oppressive as if a storm were about to burst.

Adelle approached the mirror, boldly.

'You can't stop me,' she said to the face. 'It's my life. You can't make me do things any more. I won't let you.'

The face stared back at her, equally firmly, darkly angry. The eyes flicked rapidly, downwards, focusing on something on the dressing table. Not the dolls, which had been put back on the window ledge but something else. Something more dangerous.

'I won't pick them up,' Adelle said. 'I won't. I'm in control. I'm in control.'

Chapter 8

'Good heavens,' Naomi said, the minute Adelle arrived. 'What have you done to your hand?'

'My neighbour's cat,' said Adelle, repeating the story she had told her mother. 'Nero. It's a right nutcase. I went to stroke it this morning and that's what happened.'

Naomi looked at the marks a little more closely than Adelle's mother had done.

'Nasty,' she said. 'Pretty deep for cat scratches too. Maybe you should see a doctor.'

'No,' said Adelle burying her hand deep into her pocket to avoid further examination. 'I hate doctors! I've put some cream on. I'll be fine.'

There was no way she was going near a doctor. A doctor would know what Naomi only suspected – that these were no cat scratches. They were marks made by scissors. The scissors the face had made her reach out for. It was the face's fault. The face had made her cut herself.

'Well you don't need to worry about our cat,' said Naomi, bending down to stroke a huge, hairy tabby. 'She's far too fat and lazy to attack anybody, aren't you, Tigger?'

The word fat pierced into Adelle's brain, forcing her to stand up straight, pulling her stomach in.

'Hello, Adelle,' Naomi's mother said, as they passed through the hall, on their way to Naomi's room. 'Nice to see you again.'

'Again'. Why did all words suddenly seem like weapons? A stabbing reminder that their last meeting had been in London, when she'd bolted from that shop.

Adelle tried to smile as she returned the greeting. But once in Naomi's room she felt compelled to explain.

'I'm sorry,' she said. 'I don't know what your mother must have thought of me the other week.'

'Nothing,' said Naomi, hastily. 'She didn't think anything. You were obviously in a hurry to catch your train.'

'It wasn't that,' said Adelle.

Here was her chance. A little sooner than intended, but here was the chance to open up. To entrust Naomi with a secret that would really test her friendship.

'I . . . I . . . get panicky in shops sometimes. The crowds . . .'

'Yeah, I guessed it might be something like that,' said Naomi, sitting on the end of her bed. 'Happens to lots of people.'

'And your mum didn't say anything? About who I was with?'

Naomi considered lying. Brushing it off. She hadn't intended to start their day with heavy conversations. But, on the other hand, she might never get another opportunity.

'Well, she said she knew him,' Naomi volunteered. 'Not knew him exactly. But knew who he was. From the papers and that. Politician, isn't he? She told me his name but it didn't mean anything to me. I don't take much notice of politics.'

'It's not exactly his politics that my dad's famous for.'

'Your dad?' said Naomi. 'I did wonder.'

'I changed my name,' said Adelle by way of explanation. 'I don't like people to know.'

'I'm not going to say anything,' said Naomi. 'If that's what you mean.'

'How much did your mum tell you?'

'Nothing,' said Naomi. 'Nothing much. Said she thought he had to resign a while back. Some scandal that she couldn't quite remember. Thought it might be something to do with selling illegal armaments or taking bribes.'

'Your mum was wrong... and my mum was right,' Adelle added.

'What do you mean?'

'She keeps telling me that people won't remember. That I keep hyping it up all out of proportion in my own mind. That nobody cares any more. That there have been so many scandals, it all becomes one big sleazy blur in their minds.'

'Not armaments or bribes then?' Naomi questioned.

'Nope. Not even close.'

For a while there was silence. Neither of them wanted to make the next move.

'I guess Stella and Anna have been getting to me,' said Naomi, eventually.

'Meaning?'

'They keep telling me to butt out. Stop interfering in people's lives. They reckon I do more harm than good. So these days I'm terrified to open my mouth. There's a million questions I want to ask you but I'm scared I'll put my foot in it. Upset you without meaning to.'

'I won't get upset,' said Adelle. 'I'd like to talk about it. I think I need to talk to someone outside the family. Not a counsellor or a professional. Just a friend.'

Naomi smiled at the word 'friend'. Just a few weeks ago, the idea of being classed as a real friend would have seemed impossible.

'But I wouldn't want it to get around,' Adelle added.

'It won't,' said Naomi. 'Not from me.'

'It's hard to know where to begin,' said Adelle. 'Or how to explain. I was almost eleven. In my last year at primary school. Private but mixed. Boys and girls. That's important. I think I might have coped better if it had just been girls. I don't know. Anyway we lived in Hertfordshire then. At least me and Mum did. I hadn't seen much of Dad for a year or two. He spent a lot of time in London. It was OK. He still came back at weekends, sometimes. Things were a bit strained between my parents. I knew that, but it was no big deal. Lots of kids had parents who worked away. Parents who were separated.'

'Mmm,' Naomi agreed. 'About half the girls in our class, for a start!'

'It seems a bit funny now,' Adelle continued, 'but I didn't really have a clue what Dad did. Like you say, politics isn't something you take much notice of, is it?'

'Well Mrs Trent seems to think we should,' said Naomi, changing her voice to imitate their history teacher. 'How can you expect to understand history, gals, if you've no idea what's going on in the world?'

'I didn't even realize my dad was so well known,' said Adelle. 'Apparently he was forever cropping up in the papers. The heavy papers. Stories about his work. What he was saying and doing. The tabloids didn't take much interest in him until . . .'

'What?' Naomi prompted. 'What did he do?'

'Shoplifting,' said Adelle. 'He was caught shop-lifting.'

'But that's crazy,' said Naomi. 'I mean, from what

little you've told me about your dad, his family were well rich. Why on earth would he need to nick anything?'

'He didn't need to, that's the point! Anyway the newspapers got hold of it.'

'But surely they couldn't make much out of a bit of shoplifting?'

'Think about who he was, for a start,' said Adelle. 'Sure shoplifting's not much of a story if it's your average man or woman in the street but if it's a vicar, policeman, politician . . . people who are supposed to set an example, support law and order and all that.'

'Yeah, of course,' said Naomi, feeling a bit stupid.

'And it wasn't so much the stealing, as what he stole,' said Adelle, determined to entrust Naomi with the whole secret. 'I think me, my mum, the family, might have coped better if it had been something ordinary. Tins of baked beans or designer watches. But it wasn't. It was underwear.'

'Underwear!' said Naomi, almost tempted to laugh at the thought of a top politician sneaking out of a shop with a pair of boxer shorts stuffed in his pocket.

'Women's underwear,' Adelle explained.

'Oh.'

'Precisely,' said Adelle. 'You can imagine the fun the papers had with that, can't you? Pictures of black, lacy bras and knickers. Lurid headlines!'

'Why?' said Naomi. 'Why did he do it?'

'Now there's a good question,' said Adelle. 'That's what made it such a fascinating read. Everyone had their own pet ideas about what he was up to. Some sleazier than others. A lad at school had some theories for me. A lad I'd known since infants. Someone I thought was my friend. Anyway, he brought the newspaper article in and pinned it on the blackboard. I didn't even know about it until he brought it in. My mother didn't bother to tell me,' she added, bitterly.

'Maybe she thought . . .'

'She thought she was protecting me,' Adelle interrupted. 'She thought all eleven-year-olds were as sheltered and naive as I was. That they wouldn't pick up on a story like that. But they did.'

'So that's why you went up to Yorkshire, to live with your gran?' said Naomi, trying to piece together the fragments of Adelle's story.

Adelle nodded.

'I didn't go straight away. At first Mum thought it would all blow over in a couple of days. That maybe Dad would be able to bluff his way out of it. They told me the same lie that they tried to tell everyone else. That Dad had picked up the underwear as a present for Mum. That he'd had so much on his mind that he'd simply walked out of the shop and forgotten to pay for it.'

'That sounds fairly likely to me,' said Naomi. 'I

almost walked out of W.H. Smith's with a magazine once. It's easily done.'

'Well, they had me fooled, for a while,' said Adelle. 'It wasn't easy, at school, with everyone going on about it. But I just kept repeating the story. My dad isn't a thief. He just forgot to pay. Only it wasn't as simple as that. The papers didn't let it rest, once they'd got their talons in. Someone found out it had happened before. Twice! Both times Dad had somehow managed to keep it quiet. But then it came spilling out all at once. My dad wasn't only a thief. He was a liar and a thief.'

'Surely that's a bit harsh?' said Naomi. 'Everyone does stupid things sometimes. Tells a few white lies to cover up. It's human nature.'

'It was more than a few,' said Adelle. 'The more the reporters dug, the more they found. What my dad had been doing. Who he'd been seeing. They never left us alone! They were outside the house when I left for school in the mornings and there again when I got home. Finally they ran a story about this interesting club my dad had been frequenting. And the things people got up to there! Things you don't really want to imagine your own father doing. That's when I was bundled off to Yorkshire. The whole business was getting out of control.'

There it was again. That phrase. Out of control.

'Gran tried to help me make a fresh start up

there. I changed my name. Went to an ordinary comp, in an attempt to be normal. My dad agreed to see a therapist about his little problem. Then, of course, that appeared in the papers too. I suppose the whole business was only news for a few weeks but you've no idea what something like that does to a family,' said Adelle quietly.

'No,' Naomi admitted after a pause. 'No, I haven't.'

'They tell me things would have happened anyway,' said Adelle. 'The divorce, Grandad's heart attack. But it all came at once. I couldn't cope . . . I . . .'

'Is that when it started?' said Naomi carefully.

'When what started?'

'You know, the . . .'

Naomi barely knew how to go on. She hoped Adelle would help her out. Volunteer some information. She didn't.

'Your weight problem,' said Naomi, waiting for the explosion of anger. 'I mean, I expect it's a dodgy thyroid or something but I did sort of wonder whether it might be a stress thing.'

'Not thyroid,' said Adelle. 'But, yeah, I guess it could be down to stress. Comfort eating. I'd wake in the night with these terrible dreams. Sometimes I'd scream out for Gran, sometimes I'd just bolt downstairs to the fridge and eat anything I could lay my hands on. The weight piled on. I don't think

I even noticed until people at school started saying stuff. I tried to diet but it was too late. It didn't make any difference. I hate being fat but I can't seem to shift it, now.'

'Adelle,' said Naomi, horrified. 'Adelle you're not fat. Surely you don't think you're fat?'

'Stop it,' said Adelle. 'Stop it! I've had enough teasing. I thought you were my friend. I thought you'd understand!'

'I'm not teasing,' said Naomi, suddenly feeling quite cold.

'You are! I'm not stupid. I've seen you all staring at me. I've heard you muttering. You were on about my weight again to Anna the other day!'

'Yes, I was,' said Naomi. 'I've been worried about you. But not because you're fat for goodness' sake. Quite the opposite.'

'Stop it,' said Adelle again. 'This isn't funny, you know. I've got enough problems without you making it worse.'

Naomi paused. Adelle really believed she was teasing. Being cruel. There was no doubting the hurt and anger in her eyes. Naomi tried not to stare. You couldn't see much, anyway, beneath the baggy sweatshirt and trousers, but it was obvious to anyone that Adelle wasn't fat. Her wrists were small and bony. Her fingers as fleshless as chicken claws. And when she got changed for games! That's when you really noticed. She wasn't simply slim.

She was thin. And getting thinner all the time.

Yet more unnerving than the decreasing weight itself was this new twist. Adelle believed she was fat. She really believed it.

Memories of a magazine article popped into Naomi's mind. An article she'd read a couple of months back. Case studies of two girls. She'd thought about Adelle at the time, but, somehow, the symptoms hadn't quite seemed to fit. She'd allowed herself to be misled by Stella and Anna's theories about glands and hormones. Stupidly, she'd missed all the clues.

Now it all seemed so obvious. The girls in the case study had an eating disorder. Anorexia Nervosa. And, although their stories were different, they had the same common factor. The one that Adelle had just revealed. Painfully thin, yet believing they were fat.

Adelle had turned slightly but Naomi could still see the glint of tears.

'I'm sorry,' Naomi said. 'I knew I'd put my foot in it. It's just that, well maybe we all see ourselves a bit differently from the way other people see us. And to me, you're not fat . . .'

'Oh, this is brilliant this is,' said Adelle staring around as if she thought Stella and Anna might be hiding in the wardrobe, ready to pop out and laugh at her, to join in the fun. 'Is this why you invited me round? Is this why you made out we were friends? So you could have a laugh? A little joke at my expense?'

'Joke? No! Of course not,' Naomi said, desperately trying to rescue the situation. 'Look, I'm sorry! Whatever I say's going to upset you. So let's drop it for a bit, eh? Do something different. Go for a walk. Set up the Playstation. Try some . . .'

But she was talking to an empty room. Adelle had gone.

Chapter 9

'I've made a complete mess of everything,' Naomi confessed on Tuesday lunchtime.

'Go on, amaze me,' said Stella. 'What've you been meddling in now?'

Naomi looked at her two friends, wondering how much to say. She hadn't intended to say anything at all but she was getting desperate. On Saturday, she'd run after Adelle, tried to reason with her, tried, at least, to get her to accept a lift home. But no. Adelle had insisted she would walk the three miles to the main road and catch a bus.

On Sunday, Naomi had wanted to phone but didn't know the number. Failing to find it in the phone book she'd tried directory enquiries, only to find that it was ex-directory. Part of her was relieved. After all, what could she have said?

When Adelle had failed to turn up to school, yesterday, Naomi had worried. Now, after a second day's absence, she was in a complete panic.

'I really upset Adelle at the weekend.'

'Well, let's face it,' said Anna. 'It's not difficult, is it? She's so touchy about everything.'

'Yes,' said Naomi. 'But we've been getting it all wrong.'

'Not so much of the "we",' said Stella. 'It's you that's been sticking your beak in.'

'Fine,' said Naomi, unusually snappily. 'But remember we noticed how cagey she was about getting changed for games? And we thought it was because she was so skinny and didn't have much of a figure and stuff? Well it's not that at all. She hates getting changed because she thinks she's fat!'

'Oh, come off it,' said Anna, laughing. 'She's got less weight on her than an anorexic stick insect.'

'It's not funny,' said Naomi. 'That's exactly it! I think Adelle's anorexic.'

'Hang on,' said Stella. 'I know Adelle's skinny but that's not necessarily the same as being anorexic.'

'I know,' said Naomi. 'That's what I've been telling myself. Anorexia's not the same as being thin. It's an illness and Adelle didn't seem to be ill, exactly. Not really,' she added, as if trying to convince herself. 'But when she said about being fat! She was so convinced, it was scary! So I dug out this old magazine article and borrowed this book from the library.'

She produced both objects from her bag.

'And I couldn't believe I'd been so blind. The clues were there, if only I'd looked properly. The way she always goes off to eat lunch on her own . . . the way she pushes food around . . .'

'Yeah, but you know what it's like,' said Stella. 'You read up on something and decide you've got it! Pure hypochondria.'

'But I didn't decide I'd got it,' said Naomi. 'I'm talking about Adelle.'

'Same difference,' said Stella. 'My mum's nose is never out of medical books and she spends her whole life thinking me and our Jack have caught something terrible. You name it, we've had it. E-coli, appendicitis, bubonic plague, Green Monkey disease. Come to think of it, Jack is a bit of an odd colour at the moment!'

'It's not a joke,' Naomi said, repeating the words Adelle had screamed at her.

'OK,' said Stella. 'Do I take it you were actually stupid enough to tell her what you thought?'

'Sort of. Well yes. By accident! I'm sure I didn't actually mention anorexia. I just tried to tell her she wasn't fat.'

'And she flipped?' said Anna. 'Just because you said that?'

Naomi nodded.

'It makes sense,' said Stella. 'Anorexics just can't see that they're thin or accept the fact that they're ill, can they?'

'I've no idea,' said Anna, casually. 'I really don't know anything about it. Only what we were told in Health Ed. and I can't say I took much notice. I've never bothered with dieting, myself.'

'Anorexia's more than dieting,' said Naomi. 'It's a lot more complex, the book says. It's to do with self-esteem, as much as weight. Sufferers think they're stupid, useless, ugly, unloved . . .'

'That's ridiculous,' Anna protested. 'Adelle's none of those things.'

'Try telling her that,' said Naomi. 'She won't listen. She won't listen to anything. She's so far stressed out, she's stopped seeing straight.'

'But why?' said Anna.

'She's had a lot of problems in the past four years,' said Naomi, cautiously. 'I don't think she's told me one half of it but the bits I know are bad enough.'

'Like what?' said Stella.

Not wanting to betray secrets, Naomi picked the least damaging example she could think of.

'Like both her grandparents dying, in the space of four years. Her grandad when she was eleven and her gran only six months ago. Both of whom she'd been really close to. Her gran, especially.'

'I know stress can kick off anorexia,' said Stella. 'But bereavement . . . most people handle that. Especially if it's older people . . . more sort of expected. Even if you were close.'

'There's other stuff, as well,' said Naomi. 'Stuff she doesn't want anyone to find out about. That's what makes it so difficult. I don't know who to tell, what to do.'

'Nothing,' said Anna. 'I've told you a million times. Butt out. Leave it alone. It's none of your business.'

'I don't think you get it,' said Naomi, almost shouting. 'Anorexia's not something you can ignore.'

'Naomi's right,' said Stella. 'I'm still not convinced but if there's a chance Adelle's really anorexic, we need to do something. We need to tell the Head or the nurse or both. Get them to check how much Adelle's parents know.'

'I can't do that,' said Naomi.

'Why not?' said Anna. 'You're the one who's been wanting to interfere all along.'

'I know,' said Naomi. 'And I should have done something sooner, while I had the chance. Only I didn't. I held off. Leaving it to someone else! And now I'm stuck. I can't do anything.'

'Why?' Anna asked.

'Because Adelle trusted me. For a while. That's why! I promised I wouldn't say anything to anybody. I feel bad enough telling you two. But if her parents get hauled in by the school, Adelle will know who's set her up, won't she?'

'Well, what's worse?' said Stella. 'Setting her up, as you put it, or letting her drift on, getting more and more sick? She could end up with permanent damage to organs and stuff . . .'

'I know,' Naomi almost screamed at her. 'Shut up. Let me think.'

Anna and Stella looked at each other in the short silence which followed.

'I'll go round, tonight,' Naomi suddenly announced. 'I'll try talking to Adelle first. Then, if that doesn't work... I don't know. I'll make it work!'

Adelle sat in her familiar position, on the end of the bed, staring into the mirror. She was wearing her school uniform, as she'd done the day before. Leaving the flat both mornings at the usual time, with her mother. Allowing Mum to drop her at the bus stop. Sneaking back, ten minutes later, taking care not to be seen by any of the neighbours.

She wanted to go to school. Despite everything she wanted to see Naomi, partly to plead with her not to tell anyone about her dad and partly because she felt she'd over-reacted. Naomi, she was now sure, hadn't meant to be cruel. She'd only been joking. Trying to snap her out of her worries about being too fat. Trying to tell her, in Naomi's clumsy way, that it didn't matter. That the girls at school accepted her just as she was. Flab and all.

It was a misunderstanding. It would be cleared up when she saw Naomi. When she went to school. But the face didn't want her to go. It had made that quite clear.

It had been waiting for her when she got back on Saturday.

'You see,' it seemed to say. 'I warned you it wouldn't work out. You're too fat and stupid to keep friends for long. So we're on our own now. Just you and me.'

They had been on their own for most of the weekend. Mum had been with Desmond, round at his place, doing paper work together, allegedly!

At first, Adelle had barely acknowledged the face. She'd been so preoccupied, staring at her own reflection, wondering if there could have been even the merest hint of truth in what Naomi had said. But no. She was *fat*. Maybe not quite as gross as she had been a year or two ago, but still fat.

The face had accepted her preoccupation, for a while, placidly mocking with its own leanness and sharp, thin features which made hers more horrendous by comparison. Then gradually, it had become bored, irritated, demanding her attention, her conversation. Wanting to play incessantly, drawing her back each time she tried to move away. Forcing her to sit there day and night. Refusing to give anything in return. No clue to its identity. No hint of what it wanted, apart from . . .

The doorbell broke into Adelle's thoughts. She glanced at her watch. Almost five o'clock, already. After her usual return from school time.

The face glared at her as she started to get up.

'I'll have to answer it,' she said. 'It's probably just Mrs Cropper looking for her cat.'

The face held her, frozen, transfixed.

'I'll have to,' she insisted. 'It could even be Mum. You know what she's like for forgetting her keys.'

As she bolted towards the door, Adelle realized that it was neither her mother nor Mrs Cropper. The voice shouting through the letter-box belonged to someone else entirely.

'Adelle? Adelle? Are you there? It's me. Naomi.'

'Go away! I can't talk to you. Not now.'

'Why? I won't stay long. I promise. Just let me in.'

Adelle heard the door opposite opening. Heard Mr Ahmed talking to Naomi.

'It's OK,' Naomi told him. 'I think she was asleep. She's coming now.'

It was easier to open the door than wait until every neighbour in the block had gathered to watch the proceedings.

'Friend from school,' Adelle informed Mr Ahmed, to put his mind at rest.

'Are all the neighbours that nosy?' Naomi whispered as Adelle closed the door.

'Most of them,' said Adelle. 'And most of the time, I'm glad of it. Makes me feel more sort of safe when I'm here on my own.'

'Must be tricky when you're bunking off school though,' said Naomi, staring at Adelle's uniform.

'So you came to preach at me,' said Adelle as Naomi drifted towards the bedroom. 'No! Not in there. We'll go in the lounge. Do you want a drink or anything?'

Naomi shook her head.

'And I didn't come to preach, I came to apologize. I sort of guessed I was the reason you hadn't come to school.'

'No,' said Adelle. 'It was nothing to do with you. Not really. I . . .'

'I haven't said anything, you know. About your dad or where you live and stuff. And I won't either.'

'I know that,' said Adelle, surprised to find she actually believed it. 'I've told you. It's nothing to do with what you've said or done.'

'What then?' said Naomi. 'How come you're not at school? Is someone in there?' Naomi added, as Adelle glanced nervously towards the bedroom.

'Not really. I can't tell you. Not here. Are you in a hurry to get back? Can we go for a walk or something?'

Naomi agreed without hesitation, not least because she was desperate to get out of the flat. The atmosphere was somehow tense and stifling, as if the whole room was tingling with static electricity.

They ended up sitting on a broken bench on one of the grassy patches which had been thoughtfully provided to divide up the sprawling estate. Every few minutes a football would land beside them or a hungry dog would come scavenging at their feet, picking up bits of discarded hamburger and pale, soggy chips.

'So?' said Naomi, attempting to ignore the small boy who was scrambling under the bench, trying to retrieve his ball.

Adelle looked at Naomi, started to open her mouth and closed it again.

'Just start by telling me why you haven't been in school,' said Naomi. 'Are you ill? Is it something to do with your dad?' she prompted as Adelle failed to respond.

'It's . . . it's not easy to explain.'

'You said something the other week about not being in control,' said Naomi, trying another prompt.

The effect was immediate, like switching on a light bulb.

'I'm not,' said Adelle. 'Not any more. I thought I was. I thought I could handle it. But it's taking over.'

Naomi felt certain she'd made a breakthrough, that Adelle was leading on to her weight problem. So Adelle's next words came as a complete surprise.

'Remember I asked you if you believed in the supernatural?'

Naomi nodded, trying to look impassive.

'Well do you? Do you believe there are things that we just don't understand? Things outside our normal senses? Because if you don't, this is going to sound crazy. Maybe it is crazy. Maybe I'm crazy.'

Adelle had begun to speak so quickly that she did, in fact, sound a little short of sanity. She paused for a second. Not long enough for Naomi to reply.

'When my gran died I inherited that mirror you saw in my bedroom . . .'

Naomi felt her temperature bounce from hot to freezing and back again, several times over, as Adelle spoke. Whether or not the mirror was haunted, whether or not a face appeared, whether or not it was controlling Adelle's life, there was no doubt that Adelle believed it all. No wonder she looked so tense and pale!

'And I see it, it's with me all the time, now,' Adelle was saying. 'It makes me do things I don't want to do, say things I don't want to say. It's taking over.'

Naomi stared, silently. For once in her life, she was utterly speechless.

'I shouldn't have told you,' Adelle said. 'You'll say what Mum said. That I'm making it up. For attention. That it's all in my mind. Like before.'

Hard for Naomi to deny. The thought that Adelle was slightly mad had crossed her mind a hundred times, as Adelle spoke. But as the story progressed another theory had formed, based on something she'd read recently in the library book she'd got out on Saturday, after Adelle had left. She couldn't remember it properly. Couldn't be sure.

But it was enough to reinforce her anorexia theory, to convince her that Adelle wasn't crazy. Ill maybe, but certainly not crazy.

Naomi paused, for a moment, before she finally spoke. Forming the words in her mind before she let them out. Knowing that her words had a habit of taking on a life all of their own, of rearranging themselves to convey an entirely different meaning from the one intended.

'No. I don't think you're mad or making it up. In fact, I've got an idea. Let me tell you a story. Just a story, OK. See what you make of it.'

Clawing in her memory for the details, Naomi began.

'There's this girl . . . Beth.'

'Is this someone you know?' said Adelle.

'No, but it's a true story.'

She didn't tell Adelle it was a case study she'd read about in her book. A study of an anorexic.

'Beth's parents were worried about her because . . . she wasn't looking at all well,' said Naomi, choosing her words carefully. 'Her behaviour had changed too. She insisted on doing all the shopping, choosing a limited range of food and cooking the family meals, though eating very little herself. She even made lists of foods and their calorie values.'

'Who told you?' said Adelle. 'Who told you about my scrapbook?'

'Nobody,' said Naomi, gently. 'I didn't even know you had a scrapbook. I'm not talking about you. I'm not even saying this is anything like you, all right? This is about Beth. So she starts to lose weight and her parents are frantic. Mealtimes get to be a battle zone. Parents yelling, Beth throwing stuff around, younger sisters crying, until finally, Beth's parents decide it can't go on and they get Beth to see a therapist.'

'You're just like my mother,' said Adelle, standing up. 'She's always on about doctors and counsellors. Well I'm not seeing one!'

'I'm not asking you to!' said Naomi. 'It's none of my business what you do or who you choose to see. I've told you. This isn't about you! Come on. Sit down. Let me finish.'

Adelle sat down, glancing nervously around. These days she could see the face, feel its presence, even when the mirror was miles away. And it didn't like this. It didn't like this at all.

Chapter 10

'Anyway,' said Naomi. 'When Beth saw the therapist, she told him something that she hadn't told her parents. Hadn't told anybody. She told the therapist about the dragon.'

'Dragon!' said Adelle, smiling, in spite of herself. 'I thought this was supposed to be a true story?'

'It is,' said Naomi. 'It wasn't a dragon exactly but Beth reckoned there was this thing. This small, scaly, red thing with a long rubbery nose. More of a cross between a miniature dragon and an anteater, really.'

'Oh, that's OK then,' said Adelle. 'Perfectly normal.'

'And the dragon-thing,' Naomi continued, ignoring the interruption, 'was always with her, checking up on what Beth ate, what she did. Telling her when her work wasn't good enough, or when she was looking grotty or fat. It was the dragon-thing which shouted out at mealtimes and made her throw plates across the room. Beth was becoming anorexic, but she couldn't help it because the dragon-thing was in control.'

Naomi had paused after the word anorexic,

noticing a sudden, sharp glance from Adelle.

'And what did the therapist have to say about the dragon-thing?' Adelle asked, intrigued.

Naomi thought, carefully, before speaking. She wasn't quite sure about the next bit. About what exactly she'd read.

'I think the therapist said that the dragon-thing was Beth's other voice. Her anorexic voice,' Naomi added, hurriedly moving on. 'And he said it was OK for the dragon-thing to come to the sessions but it was Beth he wanted to talk to. So if it started sticking its rubbery snout in, it would have to go.'

'And what happened?'

'Well, it stuck its snout in quite a lot, at first,' said Naomi smiling, trying not to sound too heavy, too serious. 'It was stronger than Beth, apparently. It had a louder voice. The voice that Beth listened to. The one which told her she was fat and useless and ugly.'

'OK, OK, I get the picture,' said Adelle, irritably. 'I want to know how it ended up. Did they get rid of it? Did Beth get better?'

'In the end, the therapist got sick of it interfering and it was tricky because he couldn't actually see it himself.'

'You don't say!'

'So he got Beth to draw it for him. And each session after that, the drawing of the dragon-thing sat on the table. But if it got too pushy or too loud, if it wouldn't let Beth speak for herself, it was put away in a cupboard or banished to another room, so the therapist could speak to Beth on her own.'

'And Beth fell for that trick, did she?'

'I don't think it was a trick,' said Naomi. 'I think the therapist understood that although the thing was invisible to him, it was real enough to Beth. He just helped Beth to keep it under control.'

Under control. The words jolted Adelle out of the story, back to her own reality.

'So you're saying that Beth's dragon-thing is like my face in the mirror?'

'I don't know,' said Naomi, truthfully. 'I'm saying that these voices, these dual voices are more common than you'd think. It doesn't mean you're crazy or anything. It's just the mind's way of coping with stress.'

'But the mirror doesn't have a voice,' said Adelle. 'I never said it could speak!'

'It speaks to you, in a way, doesn't it?' said Naomi. 'You said you always know what it's getting at, what it means. That it reminds you how fat you are and gets you to do things you don't want to do. Isn't that what you've just told me? Isn't that like Beth's dragon?'

'No! It's different,' said Adelle. 'It's not some stupid red scaly thing. It's a face. A person. It's there. It's real.'

'Beth's was real to her,' said Naomi hurriedly,

forgetting to be tactful. 'And there was this other case. A boy. Slightly different because he was a compulsive over-eater but —'

'Hang on,' said Adelle. 'So how come you're such an expert on eating disorders all of a sudden?'

'I'm not,' Naomi protested. 'I got interested 'cos of a magazine article I read. Then I got this book out.'

'Because of me?' Adelle said, not knowing whether to be angry or flattered. 'Because you've got this stupid bee in your bonnet about me being . . . like Beth!'

She couldn't bring herself to say the A-word.

'But it's crazy. Surely you can see that? I'm not like Beth. I'm not ill. I'm not thin. I'm not losing weight. I don't throw plates around. I might have problems but they're nothing to do with eating disorders. Let me spell it out for you. I DON'T HAVE AN EATING DISORDER. Droning on about dragons and people starving themselves is just confusing the issue.'

'OK,' said Naomi, unnerved by Adelle's increasing agitation. 'But we've still got the problem of the face. Whatever it is, wherever it's coming from. You could try doing what Beth did. Try shutting it away.'

'That's what we did at first. Me and Mum. But I've told you. It's too strong now. If I hide it, if I try to ignore it, I get fretful. I start feeling ill. I can't function without it.'

Naomi barely knew what to say, any more. This was no ordinary problem. She was way, way, out of her depth. How could she help if Adelle kept on denying the basic weight issue? How could she get someone else to help, without betraying Adelle's trust?

Why wasn't Adelle's mum doing something? Surely she could see? It wasn't only the twig frail limbs. Adelle's face had changed over the last couple of weeks from being thin and pallid to positively gaunt with huge panda circles under eyes so dull they seemed to lack all natural colour.

Another theory had just dropped into Naomi's brain when Adelle spoke again.

'There's something I haven't told you.'

Naomi wasn't sure she wanted to hear but Adelle went on anyway.

'I was going to, but then you started on about Beth and I got distracted. The thing is . . . the thing is, you're wrong about the face. It's not an inner voice. It's not like the dragon.'

'How can you be sure?'

'Because it's external, not internal. It's not part of me. It's someone else.'

'Who?' said Naomi.

'It's my turn,' said Adelle. 'You told me a story and now I've got one for you.'

Naomi shuffled on her seat. The grass had emptied. The boys, even the scavenging dog, had gone home. It was getting cooler and a light drizzle had started to fall.

'One of the things that worried me about the face,' Adelle began. 'One of the things which worried me right from the start, which made me keep going back to it, was the familiarity.'

Naomi thought she could explain the familiarity but kept quiet.

'Even when it was blank, nothing more than a vague shape, it had a quality to it. A quality I was supposed to recognize. At first, I thought it was something to do with Gran . . . her ghost, her spirit,' she added, faintly. 'But then I realized it wasn't. It couldn't be. It was nothing like her. The way it frightens me, the way it manipulates, the way it plays. It likes to play games, you know.'

Naomi did know. Adelle had mentioned the games.

'It likes to play with those dolls,' Naomi said. 'The Smiddles. The ones I picked up that time. Cute little things.'

'That's it,' said Adelle, suddenly more animated than Naomi had ever seen her. 'So I started to ask myself, why? Why the dolls? There was a story. A story Cousin Julia used to tell me and I drove myself mad for ages, trying to remember it. Putting together snippets, never quite getting the whole picture. I even phoned her once, but her boyfriend said she was working in America for a month.

Anyway, in the end, I didn't need to ask. It came back to me. On Sunday night. I was lying in bed, brooding, as my mum puts it, and suddenly I remembered.'

She looked at Naomi, triumphantly, as if she too ought to remember.

'And?' said Naomi, as Adelle fell silent.

'Oh, yes. The story. Ages ago, in the nineteenth century, when the house was first built, my family, my ancestors, were well rich. I mean seriously, mega rich. Great-Great-Grandad, or whoever it was, owned three big factories. So, of course the house had dozens of servants and one of them was a maid, called Lucy.'

'Like the doll?' Naomi said.

'Exactly,' said Adelle. 'Cousin Julia named the doll to go with the story. That's how I came to remember. I just lay in bed, clutching the Lucy doll, forcing myself back to the day when Julia came into the attic, when I was playing. I guess I must only have been about six years old.

'"That one's not called Kylie, she's Lucy," Julia said, picking up the maid doll.

'"How do you know?" I asked.

'"Because Kylie's a modern name, stupid! And besides, she looks like Lucy. The real Lucy. The maid who used to work here. In the old days. Sleeping here, in this very attic, which used to be the servants' quarters. Poor little Lucy."

'"Was she very poor?" I remember asking.

'"I expect so. I expect she came from a really poor family with loads of kids. That's why she had to start working here, when she was only twelve. Hasn't Gran told you about her?" she asked in her sly Julia way.

'I shook my head. Eyes already out on stalks. I knew what my cousins' stories were like.

'"No, well, she probably thinks you're too young so I won't . . ."

'"No, tell me, tell me."

'I fell for it every time. Begging them to tell me tales that would keep me awake for nights on end.

'"Well," said Julia. "Poor little Lucy wasn't very bright but she was ever so pretty. In a frail, flimsy sort of way. Masses of blond curls which she had to keep tucked away under her cap. Well, the housekeeper could force Lucy to hide her curls but she couldn't do anything about the eyes. Huge marine blue eyes with great long lashes, much darker than her hair. By the time Lucy was fifteen, the housekeeper had a full-time job, keeping the boys away from her."'

Adelle paused and looked at Naomi.

'I don't think I understood, at the time. I was only a kid. That's why I think I found it hard to remember the details, at first. I'd buried it real deep. But it was all there, still, in my subconscious.

'"Anyway," my cousin went on. "Scaring away

lads was easy enough but there was nothing the housekeeper could do about the Master. One of our wicked ancestors. He soon set his sights on pretty little Lucy. Well, months passed and Lucy must have started to notice a few changes."

'"What sort of changes?" I asked.

'"Told you you were too young," Julia sneered. "Knew you wouldn't get it."

'"Get what?"

'"Lucy was pregnant, dumbo. She was going to have a baby, wasn't she? And, in those days, it was real bad news, if you weren't married. She'd be thrown out. Lose her job. Her home. Everything."

'"That doesn't sound very nice."

'"Of course it wasn't nice," Julia snapped. "Imagine how the poor girl must have felt. Trying to make her apron hang loose over the bulge. Trying to hide the ever growing lump," she said, picking up the doll, flapping the apron around, by way of illustration.

'"So what happened?" I asked.

'"The housekeeper confronted her and two hours later, Lucy disappeared."

'"Did someone murder her?" I said, knowing how my cousins' stories usually involved at least one body being cut into tiny pieces and served up in a stew.

'"No, silly," Julia said. "No-one knew what had happened. They sort of guessed she'd run away."

'"And did they look for her?"

'"You really are thick, aren't you, 'Del? Can't believe you're our cousin, sometimes. Lucy was a servant. A maid. Lowest of the low. Why should anybody look for her?"

'"Oh," I said, slightly disappointed. I'd come to expect something far more dramatic from my cousins' stories than a runaway maid.

'"They found her quite by accident, in the end," Julia said. "Come here."

'She took my hand and led me through the attic maze to a green door.

'"Do you know why this is kept locked?" she said. "Do you know why we're not allowed in there?"

'"Yes," I said, proudly. "The floorboards are rotten. It's dangerous."

'"Poor, dim 'Del," she said. "Believe anything, wouldn't you? It's kept locked because that was Lucy's room. Through that door, 'Del, is a tiny room. In the tiny room is an even tinier door which leads right into the eaves. It's very low in there. Very dark. Beams brush against your head when you crawl in and spiders scurry across your face."

'I shuddered. I remember shuddering. This was getting more like a Julia story.

'"Nobody usually went into the roof space," Julia whispered. "No need, you see. Nothing there except for a couple of big trunks pushed right to the back. So they got a new maid, to replace Lucy. Put her in the same room and it was ages and ages before she noticed the smell."

'"What kind of smell?"

'"A dreadful smell," Julia hissed. "Rotting meat. clogged drains, rancid cheese. All mixed together sort of smell. Of course no-one took much notice of the new girl's complaints, at first. After all, she was only a maid, so why should anyone care if her room was a bit smelly? But then, she began to complain about other things."

'"What sort of other things?" I asked, completely mesmerized, by that point.

'"Faint cries, in the middle of the night. Bony, ice-cold fingers touching her face as she slept! And, by that time, the smell had started to work its way though the house. A servant, a manservant, was sent into the eaves to check for dead rats or pigeons. But it wasn't trapped animals he found."

'Julia paused for effect. She always knew how to get me worked up.

'"At first he didn't find anything. Handkerchief wound round his nose to stop himself retching, he tried to trace the direction of the smell. That's when he noticed that the lid of one of the large trunks wasn't quite fastened. The lid creaked as he slowly began to lift it and inside . . ."

'"It was Lucy, wasn't it?" I squeaked.

'"What was left of Lucy! No-one really knew what had happened. Had the silly girl hidden herself away in the trunk and got trapped inside? Had she deliberately curled up in there slowly dying of starvation or... or, had someone killed her and dumped her body? I'm not sure anyone much cared, save to get rid of the smell. But they never could."

'"What do you mean?" I asked.

'"They cleared away the body, disinfected the room, but the smell, the wailing, the ice-cold fingers in the middle of the night remained. Nobody would sleep in there. Nobody. So in the end they simply sealed up the room. And that, 'Del sweetie, is why we're not allowed in there."'

'She told you all that?' Naomi blurted out, once she was sure the story had ended. 'Your cousin Julia told you all that when you were just six years old? No wonder you're... no wonder your imagination works overtime!'

'Yes,' said Adelle. 'But don't you get it? This isn't imagination and it's got nothing to do with eating disorders. The face in the mirror is Lucy. I'm sure of it.'

Chapter 11

'Hang on a minute,' said Naomi, brushing damp hair from her face. 'So you think the face in the mirror is a ghost? Well, OK. I'm open minded. I wouldn't like to say, for definite, that it isn't. But Lucy's ghost! No way. It couldn't be. Think about it, Adelle. Lucy wasn't ever real in the first place. She never lived, she never died. She was a figment of Julia's imagination. A stupid story inspired by a doll!'

'How do you know that?' said Adelle. 'It might have been true.'

'Were the other stories you told me about true? A goblin in the cellar, wasn't it? And the giant snake that rustled about beneath the floorboards. Did you ever see that?'

'No, of course not,' said Adelle. 'Nor the enormous spider in the shed. But the Lucy story was different. It sounded as though it might be true. Those sort of things used to happen. Young girls committing suicide because they were pregnant.'

'Maybe,' said Naomi. 'But not by locking themselves in trunks! The whole thing's too gory, too sick, too melodramatic to be true.'

'But if it was, that would explain why the face looks so thin, so awful. Think of her lying there, encased in a living tomb!'

'No. Don't think about it because it isn't true. It never happened. Look, I'll prove it to you. When does this cousin of yours get back from America?'

'I'm not sure. She might be back now.'

Naomi noticed that Adelle was shivering. The light rain, which she, herself, found slightly chilly was turning Adelle blue. Poor circulation. Something else she'd read about in her book, a side effect of dramatic weight loss.

'Come on,' said Naomi. 'Let's get back, before you freeze to death.'

Adelle looked at her watch as she stood up.

'Mum should be back. You won't say anything to her, will you? About the mirror or your own silly ideas. She's forever on at me about my eating and my weight, as it is. But you're both wrong. I'm not ill. It's the mirror that's driving me crazy. It's Lucy. She won't leave me alone.'

'OK,' said Naomi, worried that Adelle was getting worked up again. 'Calm down. I won't even come in. I'll have to get back myself. If I nip down to town I'll just be in time to cadge a lift home with my brother. Then tomorrow we'll talk about getting in touch with this cousin of yours. Sorting the Lucy story out. You will be there tomorrow, won't you? You will come to school?'

No answer.

'I'll get Mum to do a diversion,' Naomi said. 'Pick you up.'

'No, I'll come, honestly,' said Adelle, hastily.

'Half past eight,' Naomi insisted. 'Be ready.'

*

Later that night, Naomi lay on her bed, cursing the unknown Julia. Cursing the whole of Adelle's family. No wonder Adelle had problems. Her young imagination fed by creepy stories, the stress she'd been under in the last few years. No wonder she was seeing things. No wonder she was ill. But what, Naomi thought, could she do about it, armed only with her book and her theories?

Confronting Julia might be the first step but Adelle needed help. Professional help. Yet the merest mention of doctors sent her screaming up the wall. Presumably because a doctor would recognize the symptoms straight away. The symptoms Adelle refused to acknowledge.

Naomi was so absorbed in her thoughts that she didn't notice when the bedroom door was pushed open and nearly leapt right off the bed as the shadowy figure hovered over her.

'Are you all right?' her mother asked.

'I was until you scared me half to death,' said Naomi, switching on the bedside light.

Her mother was gazing down at her, examining

every feature, every contour of her body, before slowly sitting down beside her on the bed.

'You sure?'

'Yes. Why?'

'I mean, I've always thought you and I were close.'

'We are,' said Naomi giving her mother a quick hug, wondering what had suddenly brought on this bout of parental insecurity.

'So you'd tell me if you had a problem?'

'Sure,' said Naomi. 'I'll even make one up, if it'll make you feel any better. What's all this about?'

'I'm sorry,' said her mother. 'I hope you don't think I was prying or anything but I came in to put some shirts in your wardrobe, this morning.'

'Thanks,' said Naomi, mechanically.

'And I couldn't help noticing the book on your bed.'

'Ah!' said Naomi.

'I mean you don't look as though you might have... but I thought... well I...'

'It's nothing personal,' said Naomi hastily. 'I don't have a problem. The book's not for me, exactly.'

She considered telling her mother that she was doing a project at school, but doubted she could make it sound convincing. Besides, she did have a problem. What to do about Adelle? And whatever she decided, she knew she couldn't do it alone.

'I'm worried about Adelle.'

There it was. Out. Confidence betrayed. Slowly, guiltily, Naomi told the story. Every detail.

'And Adelle swears the face is a ghost,' Naomi said, as she came to the end. 'But it's not. It's all tied up with the anorexia. I know it is.'

'Are you sure the weight problem's as bad as you say?' her mother asked. 'I thought Adelle looked a bit fragile but no thinner than your friend, Stella.'

'That's because Adelle hides it. She was wearing trousers and a baggy sweater down to her knees but you must have noticed her face? The one Adelle says is podgy!'

Naomi's mother nodded, thoughtfully.

'Thing is,' said Naomi, 'my book says that two-thirds of anorexics make a full recovery. But they have to get treatment. It doesn't just go away on its own.'

'And Adelle won't even consider treatment?'

'Mother!' said Naomi. 'She won't even admit she's got a problem. She's convinced she's fat. The only problem she admits to is the face and she'd rather believe that's Lucy than a feature of the illness.'

'And what about her parents, why haven't they. . ? '

'I don't know. Adelle's had nervous problems before. Maybe they think it will just go away. Maybe they're too wrapped up in their own lives. Maybe they're just not looking properly. I think her mum's tried. But the point is, if it's not caught soon . . . Did you read the book?'

'Bits of it, yes.'

'Did you read the case study of Gwen?'

'Yes. It was terrible. Poor girl weighed less than four stones when she died. But Naomi, that was an unusual case! You said yourself that deaths are comparatively rare. Especially in child or teenage anorexics, the book says. It's only a very small percentage who keep relapsing over the years.'

'And I don't want Adelle to be part of those statistics. I want her to get help. Now! Is that the phone?' said Naomi jumping again.

This whole business was making her so edgy.

'Don't worry, your dad'll get it, if he hasn't fallen asleep.'

He clearly hadn't, as the phone stopped ringing and a second or two later Dad popped his head round the door.

'Adelle's mother, for you, Naomi,' he said.

Naomi leapt off the bed and shot towards the phone.

'I'm sorry to trouble you,' she heard Adelle's mother say.

'That's OK. Is Adelle all right?'

'Well, no. She's in her room. She keeps shouting out but she won't let me see her.'

Stifled sobs filled the pause before Adelle's mother went on.

'I can't do anything! I can't even get her to open

the door. She says Lucy won't let her out. But there's no-one in there with her, I'm sure. Is Lucy someone from school? Has someone been bullying her? You've been with Adelle a lot, recently. She talks about you all the time. You seem to have been getting close. I thought you might know.'

'Where does Adelle's cousin Julia live?' Naomi asked.

'Not Julia, Lucy,' came the confused response. 'She's screaming about Lucy.'

'I know,' said Naomi. 'It's to do with a story Julia once told Adelle. Adelle thinks . . . oh, look, I can't explain on the phone. I'll come round. I'll explain properly when I see you. But, in the meantime, can you get hold of Julia? Would she be able to come over?'

'I expect so. If she's in. She only lives in Milton Keynes but I shouldn't think she'll want to rush over here. She's always so busy. What do I say? What do I tell her?'

'Tell her it's important,' said Naomi. 'There's something we need to get through to Adelle and only Julia can do it. Please. Just believe me. Just get her there.'

Naomi had no trouble persuading her own mother to drive her over to Adelle's and was relieved when her mother insisted on accompanying her inside. This wasn't something she wanted to face alone.

Adelle's mum opened the door and greeted them in a whisper.

'Thank you,' she said. 'I haven't told Adelle you're here but she may have heard me phoning you. I don't know.'

'Have you phoned the doctor?' Mrs Gardiner asked, following Adelle's mother inside.

'No. I can't. Adelle hates doctors, she'll go wild.'

'I know,' said Mrs Gardiner, firmly. 'But I think you must.'

'I've phoned Julia,' said Adelle's mother. 'She wasn't very pleased to be summoned but she's coming. I mean I couldn't even tell her why I wanted her here. What's going on?'

'It's about the face in the mirror Adelle's been seeing,' said Naomi.

'But that's all nonsense,' said Adelle's mother. 'We talked about it. She hasn't seen it for ages!'

'She has,' said Naomi. 'She just hasn't told you. It's been getting worse. Stronger. And it seems to be tied in with a ghost story Julia told her when she was little.'

'I knew it!' said Adelle's mum. 'Those flaming stories! I knew there'd be one about a haunted mirror. I've tried to tell Adelle, time and time over. They were all rubbish. Childish nonsense. Make-believe. But Adelle won't see it. She just refuses to grow up.'

Refusing to grow up. Something else Naomi

had read about in her anorexia book. Low weight was a way of staying child-like. Of stopping development.

'I know,' said Naomi. 'That's why we need Julia. To explain that this particular story was like the others. Made up. No death. No ghost.'

'And what makes you think Adelle will listen?' Adelle's mum said, wearily. 'She won't even come out of her room. There's no lock on the door but she's pushed something behind it. I can't get in.'

'Let me try,' Naomi said, leaving the two mothers together, in the kitchen. 'Don't do anything yet. Don't phone the doctor. Not until Julia turns up.'

Naomi went and positioned herself outside the bedroom door. Gave it a tentative push. Heard the crack of the door against wood. Tried to peep through the gap which had opened up.

'Go away! I've told you. I can't open it. I can't let you in.'

'It's me, Naomi.'

Slight pause, as if Adelle were checking with Lucy.

'You can't come in.'

'I have to,' said Naomi. 'I need to talk . . . to Lucy. Tell her I want to talk to her.'

It was a long shot, Naomi knew. But if she pretended to go along with it, joined in the game, it just might get her inside that room.

Longer pause. Sound of something being dragged across the carpet. Naomi pushed open the door before Adelle had time to change her mind.

All the lights were full on. Overhead light. Wall light. Bedside lamp. The last two both turned to focus on the mirror which sat on the chest of drawers.

Naomi moved across the room, walking round the bookcase, which had been pulled away from the door, picking her way over the books which had been thrown onto the carpet.

Adelle was sitting on the edge of the bed, by the mirror, trembling. Just by looking, you could tell she had a temperature. Her normally pale face was flushed, burning, dripping sweat. She hadn't even changed out of her uniform. She must have been sitting in damp clothes for three hours or more. As Naomi moved closer, she noticed something else too. There were scratches on both hands now.

In that instant, Naomi changed her mind. There was no time to wait for Julia. Adelle needed a doctor. Now.

'Be careful. Lucy's angry,' Adelle said, before Naomi could back out of the room. 'She didn't want me to tell you those things. I was stupid. I'm always stupid. I should have kept quiet.'

'No,' said Naomi, gently. 'You were right. And the face, whoever it is, is wrong.'

'Lucy. It's Lucy. I know.'

'Adelle,' said Naomi.

She paused. No point mentioning doctors. Best just to slip out and get Adelle's mum to phone.

'I . . . er . . . just need to see my mum a minute.'

'No,' said Adelle. 'Don't leave me. Don't leave me with her.'

'It'll be all right,' said Naomi, looking in the mirror. 'She's not there, at the moment, look. I think she's gone.'

'She is,' screamed Adelle. 'She is there! But you won't see her. Mum couldn't see her. Lucy only lets me see her.'

'OK,' said Naomi, staring at the mirror, again, seeing only herself and Adelle. 'Can you still see her?'

Adelle nodded.

'Describe her for me. So I can sort of imagine her,' said Naomi, trying to keep Adelle occupied until Julia turned up or Adelle's mum came in.

'I told you,' said Adelle.

'You said it was a proper face now. Not just a shape or faint lines. But you never described her exactly.'

'She's got blond hair,' said Adelle, sullenly.

'Like yours?'

'No,' she snapped. 'Nothing like mine. Lucy's is very thin, wispy, lifeless, like it was when they found her.'

'And the eyes?' said Naomi. 'What colour are they?'

'Hard to say. They're so pale. Greyish, I think. Or green. Why? Why does it matter?'

'It doesn't,' said Naomi, hearing the ring of the doorbell. 'But what if the face isn't Lucy? What if I could prove it isn't?'

'You can't,' said Adelle.

'Maybe not me but . . .'

''Del, sweetie,' said a voice from the doorway. 'What is it? Your mum said you're not too well. Gosh, you look terrible!'

Chapter 12

Julia didn't look particularly wicked, Naomi thought. She was tall, sophisticated, immaculately dressed. She had short, blond hair and a pleasant smile, resting on a moderately pretty face. But then, most people change as they get older. Grow up. She probably hadn't meant to terrify Adelle nine years or so ago.

'I'm not sure why your mother wanted me to come,' Julia began as she moved towards them. 'I mean I'd love to help but I can't see what I'm supposed to do. She seemed to think you wanted to talk to me about something but I think the talking should wait. You need a doctor . . .'

'No!' Adelle screamed. 'I'm not ill. I'm not ill.'

'Hey, steady on, 'Del,' said Julia.

'You told Adelle a story once, about a maid,' said Naomi, hastily, now desperate to get this over with, to try to make Adelle see sense. She picked up the Lucy doll. 'About a maid called Lucy. Do you remember?'

Julia looked at her, as though she was mad.

Naomi was aware of two figures standing in the doorway, behind Julia. Adelle's mum and her own.

'Do you remember the story?' Naomi persisted.

'Yes, of course!' said Julia, smiling in a bemused way. 'But what's that got to do with anything?'

'I want you to tell Adelle it wasn't true,' said Naomi, urgently. 'Tell her you made it up, like all those other stories.'

'Why?' said Julia, looking from Naomi to Adelle and back again. 'What's going on?'

'Just tell her,' Naomi insisted. 'There was no maid, was there? No trunk. No decomposing body.'

'Er no, of course not,' said Julia, still looking, suspiciously, at Naomi. 'I made it up.'

'Is that true?' said Adelle. 'No, don't look at Naomi. Never mind what she wants you to say. Just tell me the truth.'

'It is the truth, sweetie,' said Julie. 'There was no Lucy. No rotting body in a trunk. It was just one of my silly stories.'

'No!' Adelle screamed, her whole body shaking. 'Lucy's real. She's there. She's there now. I see her. I see her.'

'See her?' said Julia, incredulously. 'You see Lucy? Oh, 'Del, that's cr . . .'

Naomi glared at Julia.

''Del, love,' said Julia, quickly changing what she was going to say. 'I don't pretend to know what's going on or what you think you're seeing. And I'm sorry if I ever upset you . . . but honestly,' she said, glancing at Naomi again, 'it can't be Lucy. There isn't any Lucy. Never was.'

'Now, wait a minute,' said Adelle's mother, moving into the room until almost level with Julia. 'This maid story...'

She stopped as her eyes passed beyond Julia to Adelle. To the shivering body, the heightened colour, the scratches.

'Oh, no! Adelle!'

She rushed up to her daughter and flung her arms round her.

'Mum,' said Adelle, starting to cry. 'Help me.'

A fortnight later, Naomi raced along a hospital corridor. She didn't need to read the signs. This was her third visit. She knew the way.

It was two weeks, exactly, since the night she'd been summoned to Adelle's. Hearing Julia's repeated assurances that Lucy was no more than a myth had, eventually, calmed Adelle but the knowledge alone couldn't bring down her temperature or restore a year's lost weight.

Even with the temperature, hysteria and scratches, Adelle's mum had been, strangely, reluctant to call the doctor. She seemed terrified of upsetting her daughter, seemed desperate to believe Adelle's pleas that she'd be fine again in the morning.

In fact, it had been Naomi's mother who'd

called the doctor in the end. Adelle, true to her threats, had gone wild but by the time the doctor arrived, all her energy had drained and she lay, as meekly as a rag doll, while the doctor took a look. Not that anyone would have to look particularly hard. The high temperature and self-inflicted marks had been enough to get Adelle admitted to hospital straight away.

As soon as Adelle's father had been informed, he'd had her moved to a private ward and insisted on paying for all manner of specialist treatment.

Guilt money, Naomi had thought, but her mum had said that was unfair. That Adelle's parents simply hadn't realized quite how ill their daughter had become. That they'd only wanted what was best for her.

Naomi wasn't convinced but she didn't have time to think about it now. Her first visit had been a disaster. Adelle had screamed at her, blamed her, accused Naomi of letting her down. Naomi wondered how she'd ever plucked up courage to go back a second time. Stella and Anna had advised against it.

'You've done everything you can, Naomi. Let it go.'

'I can't. You don't just dump on your friends when things get a bit tough.'

'I don't know why you're bothering,' Anna had said. 'I mean she's not exactly a bundle of fun to be around, even on a good day.'

'That's where you're wrong,' Naomi had insisted. 'When you get to know her, when you get her talking, get beyond the illness, she's fine. There's even a great sense of humour under that screwed-up exterior. If she can just get through this. Get back to normal. You'll see.'

'You're mad, Naomi,' Anna had said, though not unkindly. 'Completely bonkers. She doesn't appreciate any of this, you know. She'd be far happier left to wallow in her own misery.'

'Rubbish!' Naomi had argued. 'She doesn't want to be miserable and she doesn't want to be anorexic, any more than you want that cold you've got or I want my freckles. And she can't help it! This isn't something she's chosen, you know.'

Her friends had remained sceptical but Naomi was glad she'd ignored them. On the second visit, Adelle had seemed pleased to see her. Very quiet. Hardly spoken at all. But she'd listened to Naomi's tales of school. Even smiled once or twice.

Adelle's mother had said, on the phone yesterday, that Adelle was getting better, stronger, every minute. That, under hospital supervision, there'd been slight improvement in dietary intake, whatever that was supposed to mean. Full recovery, Adelle's parents had been warned, would be slow. They would have to be patient.

And now the third visit. How would that go?

Naomi approached the bed, slowly, trying a hesitant sort of smile. She wasn't sure what sort of mood would greet her. The appearance of the mirror, on the bedside table, surely wasn't a good sign.

'Hi,' she said, dumping a paper bag in front of Adelle. 'I know you don't like grapes and you've got enough flowers to open a shop, so I've brought you a book.'

'It's not about eating disorders, by any chance, is it?' said Adelle, smiling.

'No! It's a sort of Sci-Fi comedy thing. Thought you could probably do with a bit of a laugh stuck in here.'

'It's not too bad,' said Adelle. 'But I feel a bit of a fraud, now. My temperature's down, the blood tests were normal. I feel perfectly OK. I'm just taking up a bed. But they won't let me home yet.'

'You've probably got to build up your strength.'

'Weight,' said Adelle. 'The nurses put it a lot more bluntly than you did. They won't let me out until I've put on a bit of weight and then I'll have to come back each week as an outpatient. It's stupid. Look at me! I've already put too much weight on.'

Naomi refused to comment. Refused to be drawn into an argument about Adelle's weight, which didn't seem to have changed much at all. That was best left to the professionals. But she couldn't help glancing towards the mirror.

'I asked Mum to bring it,' said Adelle. 'My therapist said I could. She wants to see it, for herself. Have I told you about Ingrid?'

Naomi shook her head.

'I've seen her three times. She's Scandinavian or Dutch or something, I think. Lovely voice! "I vud like to see your mirror," ' said Adelle, making Naomi laugh at her dreadful attempt at a foreign accent.

'You've told her about the face, then?'

'Yeah,' said Adelle. 'And she obviously reads the same books you do. She was completely unfazed by it. "Ah! Zat vill be your anorexic voice!" '

Adelle paused. She had taken herself by surprise. She had said the word. The A-word.

'In a way,' she told Naomi, 'I wish I'd met Ingrid sooner. The way she accepts everything makes me feel positively normal.'

'You are normal.'

'Compared to most of her clients, obviously. I bet they see dragons, ghosts, anteaters and all sorts! I wish you could meet Ingrid. You'd like her. She's so patient. So laid back. I can't seem to do anything wrong, in her eyes. If I yell at her, she just says, "Ze face is back, is it not? I can hear it. Frightening you. Making you say zese things." And she turns the mirror round to the wall.'

'And does it help?' asked Naomi, cautiously.

'I think so. The other day Ingrid was trying to get

me to look at the eating plan the dietician's drawn up. For when I go home. Well, I got really worked up because it was full of dead fattening things. I mean, I've been trying to eat. Trying to do what they say. But she was talking about bread and pasta! I started shouting and she smiles and says, "Excuse me. I can't hear vat Adelle vants to say." And she shoves the mirror under the bed. I remember thinking, she's more of a loony than I am, but yes . . . it helps.'

'And do you still actually see the face?' said Naomi.

'Sometimes,' Adelle confessed. 'And, apparently, to see things so vividly is a bit unusual. Some anorexics don't have an "inner voice" at all, but a lot do. A few hallucinate but Ingrid's only ever heard of one other case like mine and she's never come across one herself . . . till now!'

'So what does she make of it?' Naomi asked.

'Oh, Ingrid's got answers for everything,' said Adelle. 'You're not going to believe this but she says it's just myself I'm seeing. But, because my imagination's so strong, I've created a split image. A fat, repulsive, useless self and a terrifying anorexic self. Neither is the real me. Thank goodness! But the anorexic self's been getting stronger. Taking over.'

Naomi didn't find it at all hard to believe. Although she hadn't seen it quite so clearly as Ingrid, she'd had a similar theory herself. From the minute Adelle had said the face seemed familiar.

''Spect it's rubbish,' said Adelle. 'I still can't believe I've got an eating disorder. Not really. But, in a way, I hope she's right. 'Cos Ingrid said once we get the eating under control the faces, the fat one and the anor . . . the other one, will start to go away and I'll be able to see the real me.'

Naomi smiled, pleased that Adelle was showing confidence in Ingrid and that the counselling appeared to be helping.

'I think,' said Adelle, 'that I sort of knew the face wasn't real. I wanted to believe it was a ghost. Gran's ghost, Lucy's ghost, anybody's ghost. Anything was better than believing I was crazy.'

'Don't say that!' said Naomi. 'You're not crazy! Stressed, angry, whatever, but not crazy.'

'Have you ever thought of becoming a therapist?' Adelle asked, grinning. 'You sound just like Ingrid. Work on the accent a bit and you'll be perfect.'

'I don't know about the accent!' said Naomi. 'But I have thought about becoming a psychologist.'

'You're having me on!' said Adelle. 'You never told me that before.'

'Yeah, well,' said Naomi, sheepishly. 'Stella and Anna sort of put me off a bit. They reckon I'm far too blunt and tactless. They think I need a job which keeps me well away from people. Working in a nice isolated cave somewhere, with a computer, they reckon.'

'They've both sent me cards,' said Adelle, picking out two from the huge pile on the cabinet. 'Everyone's been really good.'

'Had many visitors?'

'Yeah,' said Adelle. 'Only I'm not allowed too many just yet. Ingrid says we should keep them to a minimum, for the time being. Mum comes every day, of course. Dad's been twice. He'd come every day, too, if we let him but I still find... it's difficult... you know?'

Naomi wasn't sure she really understood. How could she? Nothing like that had ever happened to her. It was almost impossible to imagine how she'd react, how she'd feel, how she'd cope, if it did.

'Ingrid says we have to have some family sessions. I've got the first one tomorrow morning. Dad's travelling up, later tonight. Can't say I'm looking forward to it, but Ingrid reckons it should help. She says I still haven't worked through a lot of the anger. The grief. The confusion.'

A nurse arrived, at that point, carrying a yellow frothy drink.

'Snack time,' said Adelle, pulling a face at Naomi. 'It's one of those healthy drinks that they give people who can't eat properly. Full of yummy vitamins. You don't have to stay,' she informed the nurse.

'It's all right,' said the nurse, cheerfully. 'I'll just wait until you've finished it and take the glass away.'

'Why?' Adelle snapped. 'Don't you trust me? What do you think I'm going to do? Feed the flowers with it? Pour it in a bed pan?'

'I'm sure you won't do anything of the sort.'

'Well go away then! Go away. I won't drink it while you're standing there. I won't.'

Naomi found herself burning with embarrassment for her friend's rudeness. This wasn't like Adelle. She had been fine a minute ago. Why had she suddenly turned so abusive? Adelle would never dream of screaming at the teachers like that. But then, teachers didn't try to make her eat. Naomi realized, perhaps for the first time, how terrifying the illness must be. How strong the fear of eating. Of putting on weight.

'Adelle,' she began, but the nurse stopped her.

'That's not Adelle,' she said. 'I'm afraid the anorexic voice is speaking at the moment, so we have to wait until it goes away.'

She turned the mirror to face the wall as she spoke.

'Don't listen to her, Naomi,' Adelle said. 'She's talking rubbish. They all talk rubbish. Her, Ingrid, the doctor, my parents. They're just trying to make me gross and fat. As if I don't look awful enough.'

'You could leave it with me,' Naomi said to the nurse.

The nurse nodded, somewhat relieved, and handed over the glass.

'I'm sorry,' said Adelle. 'I don't mean to be like this, you know. It's just that I can't face it. Not today. Not now. I feel sick.'

'That's OK,' said Naomi. 'No hurry. No prob. If the worst comes to the worst, I'll drink it!'

'It's not that I've got a problem with eating,' Adelle insisted. 'I've been doing fine. I had cereal this morning *and* a piece of toast. It's just that . . . I think it's the thought of the therapy session tomorrow that's making me feel sick.'

'It'll be OK,' said Naomi. 'Come on. Let's have a look at the rest of these cards. Let's see if I can guess who they're from. Don't tell me! This one with the green monster on the front's from one of your gory cousins, right?'

The next time Adelle glanced at the clock on the wall it was turned five and the glass, on the bedside table, was empty.

'How did that disappear? Did I drink it, or did you?'

'I did,' said Naomi. 'Lovely. Banana.'

'Liar,' said Adelle, laughing. 'The yellow ones are always pineapple. Did I drink it while we were talking?'

Naomi nodded.

'You really are as good as Ingrid,' said Adelle. 'How did you get me to drink it? How did you do that?'

'I didn't,' said Naomi. 'You did. You're getting better, Adelle!'

Chapter 13

Naomi left the ward feeling more optimistic about Adelle than she'd done for a long time. A bit worried about tomorrow's therapy but she was sure it would be OK.

'Sorry,' she began, as she bumped into someone. 'Oh! It's you!'

She stared at Julia and another similar-looking girl, slightly younger.

'This is my sister, Amanda,' Julia said. 'And this is Naomi, Adelle's friend from school. Have you just seen 'Del? How is she?'

'OK. But she's not allowed too many visitors,' said Naomi, pointedly.

'Oh, we won't stay long,' said Amanda. 'We're off out tonight.'

'Only I wanted to pop in,' said Julia. 'Poor 'Del. I had no idea she was so poorly. I felt so guilty when she was raving on about Lucy.'

Good, Naomi wanted to say, but kept quiet. To start hurling blame wouldn't help Adelle.

'It never occurred to me, all those years back,' said Julia, looking at her sister, 'that poor 'Del was so sensitive. That she'd still be brooding about the story nearly ten years on. Seeing faces in mirrors!'

'She broods about all the stories,' said Naomi, bitterly. 'She's told me dozens of them. But the maid business really got a hold. She really believed it was true.'

'It was!' said Amanda.

'What?' said Naomi.

'True,' said Amanda. 'I take it you're talking about the stupid girl who locked herself and her unborn baby in a trunk and died?'

'True?' repeated Naomi. 'As in, really happened?'

'Yes,' said Amanda, smiling placidly.

Naomi stared at Amanda, then at Julia. What was going on? Surely they weren't trying to spook *her* with their stupid games. Surely they were too old for that sort of thing? Maybe they were both mad. Insane? Who could tell? Why was she even bothering to talk to them? Why was she wasting her time? They both obviously still thought it was all a huge joke.

'But,' she said to Julia, 'you told Adelle you'd made it up. I heard you. I was there. Remember?'

'Of course I remember. You manipulated the whole conversation. I hadn't a clue what was going on but it was obvious poor 'Del was in a state. Obvious what you wanted me to say, so I said it. About a dozen times over!'

'And now you're telling me something different?' said Naomi. 'Now you're telling me

Adelle was right. The story was true.'

'Yes!' said Julia.

'Rubbish!' Naomi almost spat the word at them.

'Believe what you want,' said Amanda. 'But you can check, if you like. There's even some written reference to it somewhere amongst the family papers.'

'If it's true,' said Naomi, cross at herself for continuing such a ludicrous conversation, 'then how come Adelle's mum didn't know about it?'

'She did,' said Julia. 'She'd just about made the connection with what 'Del was rambling about, when the doctor arrived. And she's given me terrible grief about it since.'

'So how come she didn't make the connection earlier?' Naomi insisted. 'When Adelle first mentioned Lucy?'

'Why should she?' said Julia shrugging. 'I don't expect she'd thought about the story for years. It's really not that interesting. Everybody in the family knows about it, but I don't expect anybody dwells on it, overmuch.'

'Except Adelle,' said Naomi.

'Yes, well 'Del was always one for fantasies. She was always pestering us to tell her stories and join in her silly games. I thought she enjoyed them! So, I guess I exaggerated a bit when I told her about Lucy. Adding a few ghostly wails and icy fingers, to pep up a rather ordinary story. I'm afraid I'm a bit like 'Del myself! Blessed . . . or cursed with a rather wild imagination.'

'Julia's right,' said Amanda. 'The basic story's dead dull. Pregnant girl panics, hides herself away and dies. We've got far juicier ones than that in our colourful family history. So I can't really understand why 'Del got so worked up about it or what it's got to do with the anorexia.'

'Listen,' said Naomi, losing patience with their flippant attitudes. 'And I'll tell you. But you've got to do something for me. You've got to tell everyone in the family, everyone who knows, never to mention it in Adelle's hearing again. Adelle's mum, everyone. And, if Adelle ever asks, they're to say what you said. It was a story. A myth. There was no Lucy. No death. No possibility of a ghost. She's getting better. Adelle's getting better and I don't want anybody screwing it up, OK?'

Naomi found Adelle in the day room when she went for her Friday evening visit.

'Guess what?' said Adelle, beaming at her.

'Er, nope. Don't know. Tell me.'

'I've reached my first weight target and they're letting me out tomorrow. Only for the weekend, to see how I get on at home. Then I'll come back in and they'll take it from there.'

'Brill,' said Naomi. 'That's really great.'

'Better than you realize. I thought I'd really

blown it, earlier in the week. After family therapy.'

'Not too good?'

'To put it mildly.'

'What happened?' said Naomi, settling down on the chair next to Adelle.

'It was OK, at first. We were talking about Gran and Grandad. How close I'd been to them. About all the times I'd stayed with them when I was younger. Grief counselling, you know? Ingrid reckons that with all the other stuff going on in my life, I've never had a chance to mourn properly. That I've kept it all bottled up.'

Naomi nodded.

'So that was fine but somehow we got onto my relationship with Mum and Dad. How I feel about Desmond and about Dad wanting to stand as an M.P. again in the next general election.'

'So what did you say?' Naomi asked.

'Nothing much,' said Adelle. 'That's the point. I can't talk about that. Not truthfully. I can't tell them how I really feel.'

'Why not?' said Naomi.

'Because they'd be hurt. And I don't want to hurt them. But when I said that, Mum started on about how I'm hurting them in different ways. By starving myself. By being ill. As if I'm doing it on purpose! As if I'm going out of my way to upset them! And before I knew what was happening I was shouting and screaming and Mum was crying and Dad was all set to walk out . . .'

'So what was Ingrid doing all that time? What did she have to say?'

Adelle suddenly started laughing.

'You're not going to believe this but Ingrid says, "This is gut. This is very gut. Ve are starting phase two, I think." '

'Phase two,' said Naomi. 'Yes, I think I read about that.'

'Proves I'm getting better, apparently,' said Adelle. 'Screaming's classed as communicating. Instead of turning it all inward. It's hard on Mum and Dad. I know that. And Ingrid's helping me to express things in a calmer way. She's seeing my parents separately too. Probably giving them tips on how to cope with a lunatic.'

'You're not a lunatic,' said Naomi. 'And you don't have to be a therapist to tell you're getting better. I can see it in the way you smile. The way you sit, even. You just look so much more relaxed.'

'Honest?'

'Would I ever lie?' said Naomi, laughing.

'Why do you do it?' said Adelle.

'Do what?' said Naomi, fearing she'd said something tactless again.

'Stick around with me? You've been so good. Coming to see me. Listening to me moaning on.'

'Stella and Anna reckon I'm doing it for practice,' said Naomi, laughing. 'Because I want to be a psychol...' She stopped, seeing the hurt expression on Adelle's face. 'I'm sorry,' she said hurriedly. 'Me and my big mouth! I was joking. Surely you can see that? I come to visit you because I care about you. I like your company. We get on well. I like *you*, Adelle. Is that so hard to believe?'

Adelle smiled but the questioning look in her eyes told Naomi that, yes, it was hard for Adelle to believe. Her self-confidence was still shattered. She'd simply stopped seeing her own good points.

Naomi was pondering about this and making a mental note to be more careful about what she said, in future, when she realized Adelle was speaking.

'Could you do something for me? A favour?'

'Sure,' said Naomi, without hesitation.

'I'd like you to look after my mirror, for a while.'

'Er, oh, yes,' said Naomi.

Since Julia's confession she'd felt a bit nervous about the mirror. Stupid, of course. Even if poor Lucy had died a grizzly death in the old house, it didn't mean she was haunting the mirror!

'Why?' she asked. 'Are you still seeing it?'

'No. No, I haven't. That's the point. I haven't seen the face for a while! And Ingrid says now's the time to free myself of it, completely, while I'm feeling stronger. Before I have to face the challenge of going home. She thinks I'll do better without the possibility of "the voice" getting to me.'

'Makes sense,' said Naomi.

'Ingrid wanted me to break the mirror, at first,' said Adelle. 'Until I told her how much it was worth! Yes, I know your mother says you shouldn't reduce things to their value in money but we're talking seriously expensive, here.'

'Sure,' said Naomi.

'So then Ingrid said I should sell it but I can't do that either. It was Gran's. She left it to me specially. I was furious when Amanda sold the painting she'd been left. Gran thought about all her gifts so carefully and Amanda got rid of hers within the week!'

Naomi listened while Adelle talked about the gifts and their meanings. Julia's ring. The pool table that was left to Nick as a hint to ease up on his studying once in a while. The carefully thought-out bequests to Uncle Roderick's three.

'So, if your gran had reasons for all the bequests,' said Naomi, forgetting to be careful, 'was there a reason for the mirror? Do you think your gran had started to notice the weight loss perhaps?'

'No,' said Adelle, hastily, trying not to snap. 'No, she hadn't. She couldn't have done. That wasn't the reason. It wasn't! Anyway, it doesn't matter. The point is that she left it to me and I can't ever sell it. I couldn't betray her like that.'

'Yeah, I can understand that,' said Naomi.

'I'm not sure Ingrid did. I swear she thought I was making excuses. But I wasn't. I want it out of the way until I'm properly better. I know I'm going to get better. I know I'll be able to have the mirror back again, some day. Hey! That's positive thinking! Ingrid would be proud of me.'

'And you don't think you should ask a member of your family to take the mirror?' said Naomi, in one last attempt to avoid having to look after it. 'After all it's a family heirloom, someone might object if I have it.'

'Tough,' said Adelle. 'It's mine. It's nothing to do with any of them. I want to give it to someone I can trust.'

'In that case,' said Naomi, 'yes. I'll take it with me, when I go.'

Why, Naomi thought, as they climbed the stairs towards Adelle's flat, on Sunday afternoon, did mothers have to fuss so much? Transforming the simple matter of looking after a mirror into a major drama.

'Darling!' her mother had exclaimed, as if Naomi had come home with the crown jewels. 'I can't just let you bring something so valuable into the house. I'll have to speak to Adelle's mother. Make sure she agrees. Talk about insurance cover. What if it were to get damaged or stolen while it was at our house? We might even have to get some sort of legal document drawn up, if we're going to keep it for any length of time.'

Before they reached the top of the stairs, it became clear that another sort of drama was in progress. Raised voices were echoing round the corridors. Familiar voices.

As they approached the flat, Naomi saw Mr Ahmed standing by his door. He half smiled in recognition, shrugged his shoulders and withdrew.

'Maybe we should come back another time,' Mrs Gardiner whispered, as the voices became clearer.

'I won't. You can't make me,' they heard Adelle scream from inside the flat.

'You've got to eat something,' came her mother's response.

'I won't eat with you sitting there watching. I'll eat it in my room.'

'That's the point. You don't eat it in your room. You hide it. I found your lunch hidden under the bed!'

'You shouldn't have been looking. You shouldn't even have been in my room.'

Mrs Gardiner looked at Naomi. 'I thought you said it was going well,' she whispered.

'It is. It has been,' Naomi replied, quietly. 'It just doesn't all happen at once. We all knew coming home would be traumatic for her. Even for a weekend!'

'You told Ingrid you'd let me eat in my room,' they heard Adelle yell. 'You promised.'

'Only as long as you were eating properly,' her mother said. 'If you don't do that, you'll have to stay in hospital. They won't let you come home!'

'Don't threaten me! I know you want to get rid of me. I know you'd rather spend your time with your pathetic toyboy. You want me to stay in hospital, don't you? . . . What's that? I can hear something. There's something outside the door.'

Before Naomi or her mother could think of moving, the door was thrown open.

'Oh!' said Adelle. 'It's you. Er, come in.'

It was difficult to say who looked more stressed, Adelle or her mother. Both were now desperately trying to appear normal. To pretend that nothing had happened.

'Tea?' Mrs Gardiner said. 'Shall I make us some tea?'

'I'm sorry,' said Adelle's mother, as Adelle turned and wandered into the bedroom. 'You must have heard. The whole neighbourhood must have heard. It's one of the things Ingrid doesn't seem to understand. She says Adelle's got to get all the anger, all the grief, out of her system before she can make a full recovery. And I know that. But Ingrid doesn't have to live here. She doesn't have to face the neighbours every morning.'

*

Naomi left her mother to utter words of comfort and followed Adelle into the bedroom.

'I'm sorry,' said Adelle.

'Don't be,' said Naomi. 'You don't have to apologize. Not to me. Nobody said it was going to be easy, did they? Nobody expects everything to happen at once. You're doing great. Ingrid says so, doesn't she?'

Adelle nodded.

'So why have you come? I mean, it's nice but I wasn't expecting a visit from the Gardiner clan quite so soon.'

'Mother trouble,' said Naomi. 'She's panicking about the mirror.'

'Why? Nothing's happened, has it? You haven't seen . . .'

'No!' said Naomi. 'Nothing like that.'

She didn't confess that she hadn't given herself a chance to see anything. That she'd wrapped it up in several layers and put it away in a box, in the cupboard, in a spare room. Pity really to hide away something so lovely, especially as it was probably perfectly harmless, but she wasn't taking any chances.

'Mum's just nervous about it getting accidentally broken or stolen. She wants to talk about the fascinating subject of insurance. You know what parents are like.'

'Don't I though,' said Adelle.

'Adelle,' said Naomi. 'Is there something wrong? I mean something more than just the trauma of coming home. You looked so relaxed in hospital. Now you're all strung up again.'

'It's him," said Adelle. 'My dad. You'll never guess what he's done now.'

Chapter 14

'What's happened?' said Naomi.

'Have you seen the news recently?' said Adelle.

Naomi had. There had been no mention of any public figures shop-lifting. No mention of Adelle's dad. She was sure of it.

'About that M.P. dying?' said Adelle.

'No,' said Naomi. 'I didn't clock that. Was it a friend of your dad's or something?'

'Not exactly,' said Adelle. 'He knew him, that's all. He was an older guy. Been ill for months, so it wasn't a shock, or anything. But the point is, there'll be a by-election soon.'

Naomi stared at Adelle, confused, wishing she'd paid more attention in general studies. She wasn't even sure what a by-election was!

'They need to fill his seat in the House of Commons,' Adelle was explaining. 'My dad's hoping to stand, instead of having to wait for the next general election. He'll be back in parliament, Naomi. The newspapers will be full of it! It's all happening too soon. I can't cope, I . . .'

So that was what it was about, thought Naomi, angrily. No wonder Adelle was having a bit of a relapse. The first weekend trial, at home, and she was expected to face this! 'You'll be all right,' she said firmly. 'You will. You'll see. It's not as though you're on your own, this time. You've got Ingrid to help. And even me, if you're desperate!'

Adelle thought about it again later, long after Naomi had gone. Maybe it wouldn't happen. Maybe her dad wouldn't be selected. Maybe they'd think he was too much of a risk and choose someone else.

'Don't worry about things in advance, Adelle,' her gran used to say. 'You spend all that time and energy fretting and, in the end, things never turn out the way you think!'

Adelle had been thinking about her gran a lot lately. The sessions with Ingrid were bringing it all out. Helping her to face the pain. To acknowledge the loss, the dreadful gap in her life, but to remember, too, all the good times she and Gran had had together. Places they'd visited, jokes they'd shared, conversations they'd had.

Remembering all the good times was helping to drive away the guilt too. Guilt about that row they'd had only a week before Gran died. The stupid row which Adelle had tried to bury in the back of her mind. The one she was learning to remember. The one which held all the answers.

★

It was almost a week before Naomi got to see Adelle again. Ingrid had felt that Adelle had got 'over-excited' at the weekend and thought it best if visitors were restricted to one, or at the most, two, a day. Naomi had been allocated Friday evening.

'Hi,' said Adelle, putting down her book and beaming as Naomi approached the bed. 'I've been dying to see you.'

'How's it going?'

'Great,' said Adelle. 'Ingrid's dead pleased with me. I've eaten all my meals, this week. All of them!'

'Brill,' said Naomi. 'You look great.'

It wasn't strictly true. Adelle still looked terribly frail but at least the dreadful greyness had gone and the circles under the eyes were fading.

'I've brought you some more cards and letters from school,' said Naomi, tipping them out of her bag, onto the bed. 'And Anna and Stella want to be included on the visiting rota, if that's possible.'

'Yeah,' said Adelle. 'It takes the pressure off Mum if other people come. Dad's all tied up in London, at the moment.'

'Any news on that front?'

'No. It's the topic of my next session with Ingrid. Can't wait!' she said, laughing. '"I vant you to think about those knickers. Ve need to confront ze underwear!"'

Naomi smiled. This was progress. Real progress.

If Adelle could joke about her dad, there had to be hope!

'So who's been on the visiting list, this week?' Naomi asked.

'Uncle Rod on Monday and Nick popped in on Tuesday, for ten minutes while Mum was here. Wednesday was supposed to be Mum again but Julia asked to come instead.'

Adelle looked down at her hands and started picking her nails, the minute she mentioned Julia's name.

'I think she feels a bit guilty,' Adelle added, still not looking at Naomi. 'Especially since she bumped into you, the other day.'

'She told you about that!' said Naomi. 'She came here to tell you about that!'

'Don't get mad,' said Adelle, looking up. 'And, no she didn't. She didn't intend to tell me anything. It was me who started it. I kept pestering her. I wanted her to tell me the truth about Lucy. I just kept on and on, until I got her to tell me everything.'

'Oh.'

'Don't look so worried,' said Adelle. 'It's all right. She didn't tell me anything new. I already knew it was true. I always did. I don't quite know how but I'd always known the Lucy story was different from all the others. And I knew Julia was lying that night. I was just too worn out to care any more.'

'Look,' said Naomi, urgently. 'True story or not true, it doesn't make any difference. Your mirror isn't haunted. I admit, even I was spooked for a while, after Julia confessed. Kept it wrapped up. But you know what I'm like. Can't keep my nose out of anything. So eventually I got it out. Had a look. Time and time again. It's in my room now. I'm keeping it all polished and nice for you. And all I ever see in it is a round, freckly face and a massive tangle of red hair. It isn't haunted, Adelle.'

'I know that.'

'So why go to all the trouble of checking with Julia?'

'I wanted to know the truth, that's all. I want to be able to face up to everything properly. So that when I'm strong enough to have the mirror back, I'll be able to say, yes, there was a Lucy. She died a horrible death, right there in Gran's old house. But it wasn't ever Lucy in the mirror. It was me.'

'That's brilliant,' said Naomi, genuinely impressed. 'That's real progress. Have you told Ingrid?'

'No, but I will. I've got something else to tell her too. Something I've been thinking about a lot. But I wanted to tell you first. You were right with what you said about Gran,' said Adelle, quietly. 'About her reason for giving me the mirror. Only I've been blotting it out. I've never really been able to face it before. Until the counselling started to bring it all out.'

'So your gran *had* noticed the weight loss?' Naomi prompted.

Adelle nodded.

'Gran noticed everything! I mean, it couldn't have been too bad, back then. In fact, at first, it was the opposite problem. What I told you about comfort eating was true. I'd definitely got a bit podgy.'

'Are you sure that wasn't just your own perception, even back then?' said Naomi.

'Yeah, I'm sure. I was doubly sure after a boyfriend kindly mentioned it! It was after Steve dumped me that I first started to diet. So, I guess about a year before Gran died I was convinced the diet wasn't working. I did all sorts to keep my weight down. Stuff you don't really want to hear about! But every time I checked, there were the same dumpy legs, puffed-up face and flabby bum! I was genuinely confused when Gran first said I was looking a bit thin.'

Adelle paused, looking down at her arms, as if she could barely believe it, even now.

'Gran wasn't one for nagging about things, though,' said Adelle. 'Not like Mum. Gran didn't try to stop me dieting but I noticed she started buying more fruit and salad, hoping I'd eat more if it was all healthy stuff...I guess.'

'But you didn't?'

'Yes,' said Adelle. 'Yes I did. I was eating. I'm

sure I was. I thought I was eating too much! I still felt fat... especially when Gran's illness started to kick in. The treatment she was having stopped working. She lost a lot of weight, really quickly. I used to sit with her, feeling gross, feeling guilty. Knowing she was dying. Knowing there was nothing I could do.'

'You don't have to do this,' said Naomi, as Adelle started to cry. 'You don't have to tell me.'

'It's not really you I'm telling,' said Adelle. 'It's myself. I need to face up to it. I need to work it through. Ingrid says talking about things, painful things, is half the battle.'

Naomi glanced round, for a nurse. She felt utterly inadequate to listen to this. To deal with it. It was all very well for Ingrid to say that but she should be here. Ingrid. Someone. Anyone. But there was no-one around and Adelle had started talking again.

'I thought I was doing OK. The family paid for twenty-four hour nursing care for Gran. I didn't want to leave her but I'd go to school. Try really hard. Bring home merits to show her. Tell her how well I was doing so she didn't have to worry about me! Show her that I was coping. That I was in control. Then one day, about a week before she died, I was sitting on the end of her bed, holding her hand. She lifted both our hands up. Looked closely.

'"Adelle," she said. "Adelle, look at this! You're nearly as thin as I am! Adelle, love, what are you doing to yourself?"

'I couldn't see it,' Adelle went on. 'I honestly couldn't. But I didn't want to argue. I didn't want to upset her. I tried to brush it off but she wasn't having it . . .'

In the pause which followed, Naomi again glanced around for help. Adelle was speaking too rapidly; her breathing was shallow, her face flushed. 'I think she knew she hadn't got much time left,' Adelle continued. 'I think she was desperate to make me understand. She told me I was getting sick. I think she even used the A-word. That's what set me off. Shouting and screaming. I said some terrible things to her, Naomi. But I didn't mean them. I didn't!'

'Your gran would know that, Adelle,' said Naomi gently. 'She wouldn't want you to go on feeling guilty.'

'I know,' said Adelle, calming slightly. 'I'm beginning to see that now. I remember going back about an hour later. I apologized. More than once. But I wouldn't talk about it. I think she was too weak to argue, by then. In the final days, all the family turned up. Swarming round. Gran and I were hardly ever alone and she only ever said one more thing about it . . .

'"Do something for me, Adelle," she said. "Take

a good long look at yourself in the mirror. Confront the problem. Stand up to it. Look it right in the face."

'That's why she left me the mirror,' said Adelle. 'To remind me of what she'd said. To try and make me see.'

'And it worked, in a way, didn't it?' Naomi ventured.

'Maybe not quite the way she thought,' said Adelle. 'Unpacking the mirror brought it all back. The row. Everything. But I couldn't face it. I didn't want to see. I didn't want to remember.'

Adelle paused, as a nurse walked past the door. Naomi stayed silent. Adelle had almost worked it through. No point asking for help now.

'When the memories surfaced, when I saw that face, I did everything I could to explain it away. To pretend it wasn't part of me. Long forgotten stories, ghosts, anything to avoid the truth. Lapsing back into childhood fantasies. Hiding, as my mum would say. Until you and Ingrid forced me to start unravelling it all. And I feel so pathetic now. So stupid.'

'No!' said Naomi. 'Don't spoil it! No negatives. You've faced up to problems most of us couldn't even imagine, let alone cope with. And you're winning. You know that, don't you?'

'I think so,' said Adelle. 'Ingrid's confident I'll make a full recovery With help, most anorexics do, you know? There! I've said the word, again! Anorexia. It's not going to frighten me any more, Naomi.'

'No,' said Naomi, smiling. 'It isn't. We won't let it.'

THE END

Author's Note

Face to Face is an entirely fictional story but the stresses and pressures which Adelle faces are similar to problems which most of us will experience at some point in our lives. Like Adelle, we may experience stress-related illnesses, especially if too many pressures pile up at once.

Most of Adelle's symptoms are those experienced by real sufferers, though 'the face' itself is entirely fictional. I haven't heard of, or read about, anyone who has 'seen' something quite so strongly. However, some sufferers do have an 'inner voice' and may give it a name, personality or form like Beth's 'dragon-thing'.

Although illness like Adelle's *is* serious, there is help available and there is hope. Many sufferers do get better. If you would like any information on eating disorders contact:

Eating Disorders Association, 103 Prince of Wales Road,
Norwich NR1 1DW
Youth Line: (tel.) 01603 765 050
Website: www.edauk.com
E-mail: talkback@edauk.com

THE GIRL WHO KNEW

Sandra Glover

'I keep seeing these pictures. In my head, on the bedroom wall, on the screen. And every time I see them, I hear Lisa screaming out...'

Paralysed in a hit-and-run accident, Kits is filled with anger – especially at her best friend, Lisa, who escaped the accident and can't even remember a single detail to help the police find the driver. But the accident has left Kits changed in other ways, too. Somehow she has developed certain *gifts* – the ability to 'dream' a future that really happens, even to read another's mind. Scared and confused, she suddenly understands that the accident was no accident and that her friend may be in real danger. Now only Kits – and her new abilities – can save Lisa's life...

'Quickly becomes a gripping page-turner'
Books for Keeps

SHORTLISTED FOR THE LANCASHIRE CHILDREN'S BOOK AWARD

ISBN 0 552 546992

CORGI BOOKS

BREAKING THE RULES

Sandra Glover

'You might as well send a shark to work in a swimming pool…'

When rebellious Suzie Lawrence is placed for two weeks of work experience at an old people's home, everyone expects the worst – she is more used to breaking the rules than looking after a bunch of ancient wrinklies.

But Suzie rises to the challenge in her own unique way, and as she fights a few battles – particularly with the fearsome Matron – everybody's lives are shaken up. Sometimes, rules are made to be broken.

'Glover handles serious social issues with a humorous touch, writes lively dialogue and has a sympathetic view of youthful idealism.'
Books for Keeps

ISBN 0 552 546763

CORGI BOOKS